A Billionaire Twist

A Billionaire Bodyguard Romance

Neve Star

[First] edition [2023]

Contents

Introduction

It is a dangerous affair, harboring feelings for someone you shouldn't, especially when she's your daughter's best friend and your best friend's kid sister.

When she brings in the latest reports, her captivating green eyes exude such warmth that when she looks at me, it puts me in triple jeopardy, shaking me right out of my tree.

Competent, wise, graceful, and indispensable; her smile and laughter fill the room and threaten to invade my heart.

In forty-three years of countless challenges, no one has left me THIS disoriented.

Being twice her age and in charge of her care, I'm to set an example; instead, I'm guilt-ridden. Torn between love, loyalty, and morality. My life has flipped. Everything's at stake. Guilty as I feel, I can't get her out of my mind nor deny the raging storm inside me.

When my daughter finds out, Olivia's job will be forfeited, and my firm's reputation threatened.

I'm teetering on the edge of a precipice from which I can't afford to fall.

Chapter 1

Olivia

Nestled on a picturesque cobblestone street, Patty's café exudes an inviting charm that beckons passersby to enter. Trailing vines adorn the café's façade, framing a small, weathered sign that bears the café's name in elegant script.

Soft, warm lights spill from the large windows, creating an alluring glow that invites visitors into its cozy embrace. As you enter, the aroma of brewed coffee and baked pastries envelops you in a comforting embrace. The inside looks rustic and elegant, with wooden beams on the ceiling and vintage artwork on the brick walls.

An antique chandelier hangs elegantly above a central communal table, where patrons sit leisurely, engrossed in conversations or lost in the pages of a book.

Patty's café has always been a local favorite, but working here was exhausting. Due to a lack of staff, the workload was overwhelming, and Patty's financial constraints prevented her from hiring more personnel.

A bead of sweat drips down my neck and onto the floor as I am cleaning. I longed for more than the monotony of this service industry, but job hunting was hard, so I made do with what I found.

"Hey, you"! A cheery voice interrupted my train of thought. It was Camila, my best friend. Her chucks make squeaky noises against the tiles on the ground as she runs towards me, hugging me.

That was Camila, abundantly affectionate. Her brown hair enveloped me and smelled of cinnamon, a sharp contrast to my red hair, smelling like coffee beans.

She pulls back, her striking blue eyes staring right at me, a smile on her face. Camila was beautiful, and she knew it.

"Come on, let's go to our spot; it's almost time." We had this routine where, at 6 p.m., we hung out in our favorite hangout spot in the café; even Patty knew of it, and she didn't have a problem with it.

I suspect it was because of Camila; Patty adored her.

As the sun dipped below the horizon, we sipped on our chai lattes while the café's chatter formed a distant hum in the background.

"God, I'm so tired of working here," the complaint slips out of my mouth effortlessly. Camila always affected me; I told her whatever I felt without her having to ask.

With a furrowed brow and pouting, she expresses her uncertainty about belonging in this job despite her love for Patty.

I'm trapped in a whirlwind of a never-ending routine". A deep sigh escapes my lips as I take a long slurp of my latte.

"I might have just the thing for you," Camila said, a sly smile on her lips.

"Really!"? I ask, almost afraid to know.

"There's an opening at my father's company as his assistant; how would you like to apply"?

"Your father's company?" I ask, my mind racing with conflicting emotions.

The mere mention of Quantum Innovations Inc. sends a shiver down my spine. It's renowned as one of the top IT companies in Chicago, a dream job for any aspiring IT student back then at the University of Chicago.

However, they select only a handful of students from the thousands of hopeful applicants each year, making this opportunity (offered to me on a silver platter) seem both compelling and terrifying.

A gnawing uncertainty creeps in – what if I can't meet their high standards? Quantum Innovations Inc. demands excellence, and the fear of falling short, of ruining this golden chance, weighs heavily on me.

Then, there's the matter of being the Personal Assistant to Camila's Dad, the CEO. That prospect alone requires more than a second thought.

Her father, a shrewd and calculated businessman, is a force to be reckoned with.

I recall the images of him barking orders to his employees, the constant presence of his pictures on the front page of popular magazines all over the city, and his sparkling blue eyes staring into nothingness.

I vividly recall the delightful flutter of butterflies in my stomach every time my gaze fell upon him as a little girl.

Alexander McQueen was undeniably handsome, a perfect blend of attractiveness and maturity. He embodied an admirable sense of responsibility and shouldered his duties gracefully and determinedly effortlessly.

After Camila's mother departed, running off to marry another man, leaving a void in their lives, he waged a fierce battle for her custody, which he won.

Despite his demanding schedule, he consistently made time for Camila. He was a skilled businessman but, more importantly, a devoted father.

But he was off limits; an insurmountable age gap stood between us, not to mention the additional complication that he was not only my best friend's father but also my brother's closest friend.

These factors, substantial enough on their own, compelled me to suppress the fluttering butterflies in my tummy, each beat of my heart echoing the longing to see his face every day and be near him.

This decision warrants careful consideration, for it's not just a job; it's an opportunity that could define my career and future.

Accepting this Job will be a medal for my poor resume excuse, and I would also gain valuable experience from working hand in hand with the CEO; it was too good of an offer to turn down.

"Hello? Earth to Olivia," Camila waves her hand before me, snapping me back to the present.

"Oh, sorry, I just spaced out for a bit," I admit, feeling a warmth creeping up my cheeks, betraying my momentary distraction.

"So, what's your decision? I can practically see the wheels turning in your head," she asks playfully, swirling her fingers in a circular motion through the air.

"I'll take it," I declare, summoning as much confidence as possible. This opportunity is essential for me; I can feel it in my bones.

"That's fantastic! I'll talk to my dad about it," she says, placing her hands gently over mine on the table, a warm smile lighting up her face. "I have no doubt you'll nail the job, Liv." I smile back at her, genuinely appreciative.

"I hope I do."

"Oh, absolutely, you will," she announces with unwavering conviction, starting to gather her belongings as she stands.

"My dad would be insane not to hire you," she adds confidently.

"Come here," she pulls me into another one of her affectionate embraces, and I can't help but playfully murmur,

"You enjoy hugging me, don't you?" Deep down, though, I cherish her hugs; they remind me of my mom's warm and loving embraces.

"What can I say," she sighs, a gentle sound escaping her lips, "you're just so adorable and tender; it's like hugging a fluffy teddy bear."

She chuckles softly, the warmth of her breath gently brushing the nape of my neck.

"Hey!" I protest playfully, pulling back from her embrace, a mischievous grin lighting up her face. Glancing at her wristwatch, she adds, "I have to go now, though."

"Sure," I say, walking with her to the door, "Bye!" She waves as she gets into her car and drives away.

I sigh contentedly, my hands comfortably nestled in my apron pockets, and I make my way back inside, clearing the table from the coffee we enjoyed together.

The café is quiet now, leaving behind a resonating silence.

I head to the locker room, which doubles as our pantry, situated behind the counter, removing the uniform I've worn all day – a simple grey t-shirt and black jeans, thankfully much more decent compared to the outrageous outfits other cafes in the area have their wait staff wear in an attempt to attract more customers.

"Long night?" Jess asks as she strolls into the locker room, her heels clicking distinctly on the floor.

I can't help but wonder how sore her legs must be from wearing those heels all day. "Yeah," I reply briefly, feeling her scrutinizing brown eyes on me.

She always seems to try to figure out whatever she thinks I might be hiding.

I wonder if she wrestles with bipolar disorder, as her mood can change drastically.

My gaze lingers on her as she sheds her uniform. Jess has a slender figure with attractive curves that give her a model-like appearance. I glance down at my body, trying to fit into my jeans that cling to my sturdy thighs. I accept and love my body, even with my thick thighs, a soft spot under my tummy, and plump flesh on my behind, although it can be challenging to find dresses that fit well.

She bids goodbye, walking confidently in a short skirt and tight top, chewing bubble gum with enthusiasm.

With relief, I mutter as I struggle into my jeans and don my black hoodie, wearing headphones despite not listening to anything. It's a little trick I've discovered. People tend not to strike up a conversation when you have headphones on, believing you're listening to music and won't be able to hear them. It's a shield against unwanted discussions. Besides, I like the feel of them against my ears.

I'm just not in the mood to talk to anyone right now, not even Caleb, the familiar figure who always occupies the doorstep of the apartment building. With a click, I shut the locker door, turned off the lights, and left the room.

"Goodbye, Patty," I say as I pass before her. She's busy with documents, likely reviewing today's sales. Her grey hair is styled elegantly, and her glasses rest on her nose. She looks up, smiles, and bids me farewell with "Goodbye, child, see you tomorrow!"

A fresh blast of cold air hits me in my face; cars drive past me so fast on the road beside the sidewalk, causing me to pull my hoodie closer to my skin. Damn it, I should have worn a shirt under this, instead of the bralette I had underneath.

"Done with work, Olivia?" I knew who it was at the first sound of the coarse and slightly scratchy voice. "I know you can hear me," he adds playfully, the sound of a basketball bouncing on the ground accompanying his approach. He catches up with me, briefly pausing the bouncing ball and cradling it in his arms.

"You know, it's not a great idea to walk this late along this deserted path at night," he advises, concern lacing his words. "What do you want, Michael?" I retort, feeling irritable.

His routine, waiting until I finish work and accompanying me home while discussing his basketball community, usually amuses me. I tease him for being such a stalker, but not today.

I'm in a foul mood; maybe my period was coming. I always have a terrible attitude during my period.

"Nothing, just walking you home as usual," he emphasizes, his tone genuine. "You should appreciate it; these roads can be unsafe."

Of course," I respond, my tone dripping with sarcasm. I'm well aware of how stubborn Michael can be. No matter how much I snap at him, he's like an unshakable shadow by my side, so I keep my mouth shut.

We cover the distance to my apartment building in about half an hour. I move to walk in, my gaze catching the space beside the cemented porch; hmmm, Caleb isn't there. However, a sudden tug on my arm jerks me back, and I find Michael's face etched with concern.

"Are you okay? I've been talking for a while now, and you haven't said a word," he inquired.

I'm glad you finally noticed, but I gently free my arm from his grip instead. "I'm all right, but I just want to sleep right now. It was nice of you to walk me home; thank you," I say, acknowledging his gesture. He nods a hint of warmth in his expression. "No problem, anything for you, Olivia.

I step into the building, exchange a nod of greeting with the doorman, and make my way up the stairs, ascending to the fifth floor. Yep, this building doesn't have an elevator. It's an old and crappy structure, and the current owner hasn't invested in renovations or adding an elevator, nor is he interested in it.

"Oh God," I gasp, feeling my breath coming in rapid, heavy pants, tiny beads of sweat forming on my forehead. I automatically place my hands on my knees, hunched over, desperately trying to catch my breath. Each inhalation feels like a struggle, escaping my lips in harsh, rugged pants as I regain my composure.

Damn, I need to go to the gym, I can't even run to save my life. I slide my key into the door lock, the satisfying click signaling my entrance. Collapsing onto my bed, exhaustion washes over me.

My eyes flutter shut despite the rational voice in my head insisting that I should take a shower. Instead, I drift into sleep, my thoughts consumed by the anticipation of good news from Camila.

My dreams carry me into Quantum Innovations Inc., and the thought of working there is a potential dream come true. If everything falls into place, it could be the opportunity I've been waiting for.

Chapter 2

Alexander

"Sir, we've arrived," Dante, my driver, announces. "Thank you," I say as I step out of the vehicle, greeted by the sight of the magnificent edifice, a tall streamlined skyscraper—Quantum Innovations Inc.

My heart swells with pride as I behold the tangible result of my relentless dedication. Since the untimely passing of my parents during my childhood, I've tirelessly labored, pushing myself twice as hard to validate my capabilities consistently.

Companies clamor to collaborate with me today, placing my firm at the pinnacle of Chicago's IT industry.

With firm and purposeful steps, I walk into the sleek building; decorative plants are placed underneath each window. The expansive reception area buzzes with prospective candidates seeking employment, invigorated by the chilly breeze from the air conditioning.

The contrast of the gray walls against the rich wooden desks harmoniously complements the architectural aesthetic.

As the premier IT firm, we encounter a multitude of hopeful applicants daily, but only a select few will earn a place within my company.

Personally vested in the interview process, I'm committed to choosing the finest candidate.

"Good morning, Mr. McQueen," Irene, my receptionist, greets me as she rises from her seat. I can sense the look of awe and anticipation radiating from the applicants' expressions, witnessing my presence. Knowing that people admire and respect me isn't unwelcome, but I try not to let it go into my head. I acknowledge her greeting with a nod, going into the elevator. It dings open, and I step out onto my floor.

My first glance at the office proves every day that this is everything I had ever imagined and more.

The main office is a modern marvel, a fusion of innovation and functionality. Nestled in a contemporary high-rise, the design seamlessly blends aesthetics with practicality. The entrance is marked by sleek glass doors, offering a glimpse of the bustling activity.

Expansive windows line the perimeter, bathing the office in natural light, while adjustable blinds provide a degree of privacy when needed.

The centerpiece is the work area, where rows of ergonomic desks host state-of-the-art computer setups. Dual monitors, high-speed connectivity, and ergonomic chairs cater to the needs of tech-savvy professionals.

Through the transparent glass, I observe the bustling tech offices—broad, contemporary desks strewn with papers, my employees passionately typing, engrossed in their computers, typing away furiously, eyes glued to their computers, already high on a copious amount of caffeine.

Meeting spaces are strategically scattered throughout the office, from casual huddle rooms for quick discussions to fully equipped conference rooms for more formal gatherings. Each area has the latest video conferencing technology, enabling seamless communication with remote teams and clients.

The well-stocked break area features a variety of refreshments, from gourmet coffee to healthy snacks, which I indulge in most times, catering to the diverse tastes of the employees. Comfortable seating encourages impromptu discussions and provides a space for relaxation, fostering a balanced work environment.

I had barely entered my office when Stephanie burst in. "How often have I told you always to knock, Steph?" She always does this, swinging my door open without knocking.

"Good morning, Alexander," she greets sarcastically. I remember when Stephanie, a childhood friend and my marketing team executive, had come to me looking for a job, and I didn't think twice about hiring her; her skills are undeniable.

I playfully tease, "Does your husband know you burst in here every morning just to see this handsome face?" as I settle into my chair, surrounded by documents. I had a habit of handling important deals personally, although it had become increasingly challenging lately. It wasn't that I didn't trust my team; I preferred being hands-on.

A scoff escapes her," Oh please, don't flatter yourself. Camila is here."

"Really?" I ask, surprised, checking my Rolex watch. It's early for her to be in the office. She had mentioned wanting to talk to me, but I hadn't anticipated this early visit. I wonder what is so important.

"Why didn't you let her in then?" I inquire.

"Oh, you know your daughter," Stephanie replies, "She insists I inform you before she comes in. She likes following protocols even when she doesn't have to."

I have always clarified that she can't expect special treatment because she's my daughter. I value treating everyone with equal respect, regardless of social class.

"Tell her to come in," I wave Stephanie away, and she leaves my office with a "Yes, boss."

"Hey, Dad," Camila greets cheerfully, a bright smile lighting up her face as she enters my office. I reciprocate, standing up from my seat and approaching her, pulling her into a warm embrace.

"That's enough, Dad," she manages to mumble, and I chuckle as I release her from my tight grip.

"You know you love my hugs," I tease, returning to my desk.

"Well, love is a strong word, but they're not bad," she says as she settles into the seat before me. I inquired about the urgency that brought her to my office so early. "What was so urgent that you came into the office this early to talk to me about it?"

"Dad...?" she hesitates before continuing, "Yeah?" I'm now genuinely intrigued, wondering what's going on.

"So, there's no other way to put this, but I need you to hire my friend." My brows furrow in surprise; that was the last thing I expected to hear, not even remotely on my radar.

"Excuse me?" I respond, genuinely taken aback. "You know we're not hiring right now, darling; no openings are available." I feel a slight pang of guilt, but we didn't need new hires.

"You're the CEO of this company, Dad. I know that if you wanted to hire someone right now, you would," she asserts matter-of-factly, meeting my gaze head-on. Determination reflects in her eyes, and I see a reflection of myself within her.

Looking at Camila is like looking in a mirror; we share the same physical features. Brown hair, blue eyes, that famous straight nose that runs in the family, bestowing us an air of distinction and an inherent drive for something better. We both share the inability to give up easily.

A sigh of resignation escapes my lips. "Who's this friend of yours?"

"Olivia." A shiver runs up my spine. It's been a long time since I heard that name and even longer since I saw the person who bears it. I knew Camila and Olivia were still in touch, considering they had been inseparable since childhood, but this was the last thing I expected, not after what happened.

"Olivia?" I ask, masking the shock in my voice.

"Yes, I met up with her the other day, and she desperately needs a job, Dad," she says, moving forward on her seat, placing her hands over mine, her eyes filled with hope, a slight pout forming on her lips. Damn, it.

"Okay," I reluctantly agree. "Yes!" Camila's excited scream fills the room as she pumps her fist.

I smile gently, focusing on the tax reports on my desk. "When would she be available for an interview?"

"Oh, right now, she's outside." Wait, what?

"What do you mean she's outside?" I look at her, noticing that twitchy thing she does when she's done something wrong.

"Camila," I call her name, a hint of warning in my tone.

"Relax, Dad," she says, standing up and heading for the door. "It's not a big deal; besides, I told her you had an opening for a personal assistant and told her to apply." With that, she rushes out of my office, leaving me speechless.

"Personal assistant?" I sputter, too shocked for coherent words. "Camila!" I yell, drawing glances from the workers nearby, but she's already out of earshot. Damn, that girl could be the end of me.

I tap the intercom on my desk and instruct, "Irene, send Olivia Dale in."

Dressed in a pale blue button-up shirt, a pair of plaid trousers, and elegant heels, Olivia stands in my office, and I find myself unable to resist stealing a second glance.

She looks remarkably different, her red hair radiating an even more vibrant hue, a perfect complement to her olive-tone skin and striking green eyes, which are now fixated on me with an expression of awe.

She's lovely, different from the image of the little girl I had in my head.

"Can I have your resume?" I inquire, my curiosity piqued. "Sure," she replies, extending a document toward me. I take it from her, my eyes briefly catching a glimpse of a tattoo on her wrist.

It's so subtle that you might miss it at first glance, but given that one of the attributes of my job is to observe even the tiniest details, I spot it almost immediately.

As I open the document, I sense her gaze fixed upon me, and the room seems to hold a palpable tension, a reflection of her nervous energy. Olivia's academic background shines through on her resume; she graduated from the prestigious University of Chicago, boasting an impressive CGPA of 4.57, and her field of study is computer technology.

However, her work experience section details stints at shopping malls and run-down cafes, a contradiction with the remarkable grade she achieved. It's clear that with such an outstanding academic record, she had the potential to land positions at top-tier companies, but her professional background doesn't align with those opportunities.

"Why should I hire you?" I slam the document shut; my skepticism is evident as I lean back in my seat, taking a moment to scrutinize her. "Sorry?" she responds, seemingly taken aback by my bluntness.

"Given your high grades, despite your limited professional experience, isn't the role of being my assistant setting you up for disappointment?"

"Working at Quantum Innovations Inc. would be a dream come true, and I firmly believe in seeking legal employment, regardless of its perceived status, Sir," she asserts with unwavering confidence.

"As for why you should hire me, let me elaborate. I possess exceptional social and communication skills, something that's in dire demand in this hub of intellectual minds you've got here.

It would be best if you had someone who can captivate your clients and infuse a hint of humor into your dealings, and I fit that profile. I'd seamlessly augment your existing workforce, and understanding the weight of your responsibilities as a busy man; I'd adeptly tackle those daunting tasks that often hinder your much-needed rest. If you bring me on board, I'll handle them efficiently and swiftly."

She takes a deep breath, gathering her pitch's final points. "And let's not forget, I'll have your coffee ready, precisely to your liking, every morning at 9 a.m., ensuring you start your day right. I'm ready to do whatever it takes," she concludes, her words hanging in the air, clearly expressing her commitment and determination.

In that instant, I see myself as a young man, and a wave of nostalgia crashes over me —a time when I, too, relentlessly pursued job opportunities from unyielding business people who showed me the door, but their resistance never dissuaded me. I endured nights outside office buildings, bracing against the biting chill until the security guards forced me to leave.

I was ravenous for success, hungry to achieve, and willing to do whatever it took. As I observe Olivia, I recognize her determination—the sincere desire to carve a meaningful path for herself. It's a rare quality that doesn't often reveal itself and leaves a lasting impression on me.

"You're hired," I announce. The joy that spreads across Olivia's face is palpable; her hand covers her mouth, and her eyes widen in sheer excitement. "Thank you so much," she manages, her eyes glistening with tears, tears of happiness, I hope.

Rising to my full height, I loom over her, my larger frame contrasting with her small, plump figure. I extend my hand for a handshake, and she eagerly clasps it, her grip surprisingly firm.

"Welcome to Quantum Innovations Inc., Olivia."

Chapter 3

Olivia

"Congratulations, girl!" Camila's voice erupts with joy over the phone. I can barely contain the bubbling excitement within me.

Finally, I've landed a proper professional job! "Thank you!" I reply, my enthusiasm spilling over as I prepare my dinner, pouring the little cereal left into a small bowl, followed by a gentle stream of milk. If you prepare your grain any other way, you're weird.

"I knew you'd get this job," Camila asserts confidently. I wasn't entirely convinced myself. I vividly recall his entrance into the reception area, exuding an air of authority that seemed to envelop him.

He embodied the quintessential image of a businessman, and I must admit, he appeared pretty intimidating.

The memory of my sweaty palms as I entered his office is still fresh in my mind. Even with the air conditioner in full force, my underarms betrayed a hint of moisture. Thank goodness for the hasty spritz of perfume before I left home. With my heart threatening to burst from my chest, that particular moment wasn't one of my finest.

Yet, amidst all this, I can recall the joy that engulfed me when he uttered those words, offering me the position.

I couldn't help but notice that he didn't seem to recognize me, or perhaps I had changed so much. The thought alone brings a frown to my face. I'm sure he did remember, but maybe he was concealing it due to professionalism.

I doubt he could've forgotten the little girl who took his laptop to a bathtub, attempting to "clean it," only to submerge it in water. I still remember the shock on his face when he caught me in the act. Instead of scolding me, he laughed heartily, his eyes crinkling at the corners.

It's a memory that always brings a smile to my face.

Suddenly, Camila's voice breaks through the trance, ringing over the phone. "We have to celebrate!" she exclaims, snapping me back to reality.

"How about we go to the club downtown?" she suggests.

"Why the hell not? Let's do it!" I reply, excitement bubbling within me. I'm ready to let loose and bask in this slight sense of accomplishment. My life hasn't looked this promising in a long while.

"Wow, you look stunning!" Camila compliments me, swaying slightly on her feet, clearly drunk. I glance down at the elegant black halter dress I discovered deep in my closet, perfectly matched with sleek black heels, delicate silver accessories, and my hair gracefully pulled up into a high ponytail, taming the curls with just a touch of gel.

A subtle touch of makeup, with a captivating shade of red lipstick on my lips, completes the look.

Camila exudes undeniable allure, wearing stylish blue pants, a sleek black tank top, and comfortable flats. I notice a blue jacket casually draped over a nearby chair, reminding me that she likely rushed here from her demanding job as an accountant at a major banking firm.

It warms my heart that she made an effort to take a break from her busy schedule to celebrate with me, yet I also can't shake the feeling of guilt, knowing how tired she must be and how much she deserves some well-deserved rest.

"Come on! Let's dance!" She exclaims, pulling me onto the pulsating dance floor, the music blasting from the speakers with infectious energy.

I laugh, mirroring Camila's playful dance moves as we immerse ourselves in the lively atmosphere. Our energetic dancing makes us break a sweat, and we eventually make our way to the bar, ordering shot after shot until our tolerance reaches its limit.

A couple of hours pass, and we stumble out of the club, flagging down a taxi. Camila takes care of me, helping me into the cab as I hiccup and barely keep my eyes open, mustering enough energy to pull her into a hug.

"Olivia, you've got work tomorrow; you need some rest," she gently reminds me, concern in her voice as she closes the door. I faintly hear her instructing the taxi driver to take me home safely. With the cold rush of air against my skin, I glance out the window, observing couples pressed against each other in the darkness.

Suddenly, I scream, "I've got a job!" before sinking into the car seat, my mind drifting into a hazy state, muttering incoherent words.

"Oh no, damn, I'm so late!" I mutter, wrestling with the crumpled blouse. It's not the ideal start to the day. After the incredible night with Camila, I was woken up by the intrusion of the morning sun streaking in through my curtains.

My eyes dart to the wall clock—8:45 AM. Panic washes over me, my throat tightening. “Where on earth is my shoe?” I exclaim in frustration.

I quickly snatch the nearest flats and slip my feet into them, grabbing my bag in a rush as I dart out of my apartment, clicking the door shut behind me and dashing down the stairs. “Hey, Taxi!”

I urgently flag one down and jump in. The time is 8:57 AM. It is official; I’m so dead. What excuse can I conjure for being this late on my first workday?

The car jerks to a screeching halt, jolting me forward, narrowly missing my head, and hitting the headrest in front of me. “My apologies, ma’am,” the driver says. “There’s a bit of traffic up ahead.” Just great. I dig into my purse, handing him a few dollars as I rush out of the cab. It’s 9:10 AM now; I glance at my wristwatch again.

Maybe if I sprint, I’ll arrive before Alexander. So I do, pounding the pavement on the bustling streets of Chicago, muttering “please,” “excuse me,” and “sorry” as I weave between the crowds of people, desperately hoping I won’t lose my job.

Gasping for air, each breath labored and wheezy, I glance at my watch again at 9:30 AM—damn, this is so bad. I sprint into the building, hearing Irene call out for me, but I tune her out, rushing straight to the relatively empty break room.

I quickly prepare a cup of coffee for Alexander, struggling to balance a couple of files on one arm and the coffee on the other.

I burst into the office, ready to apologize for my lateness, only to be stopped short by the sight of other men in suits, their expressions ranging from curiosity to irritation. My gaze locks onto

Sitting at the makeshift conference table, Alexander's gaze drilling into me with an intensity that practically scorches. “Uhm, I’m so sorry.

Please excuse me," I mutter quietly, wanting to escape this mortifying situation.

"No," a deep voice commands—Alexander. "Stand over there until we're done with the meeting." He gestures toward a corner of the office, his jaw clenched so tightly it appears ready to shatter.

The coffee in the cup burns against my skin, the heat nearly unbearable, making it difficult to hold onto it for much longer.

My arms ache from the weight of the heavy files I'm balancing, while my legs still tremble from the exhaustive sprint I made. I subtly rest my hips on the edge of his desk, attempting to regain my balance amid the room filled with the cacophony of business chatter, a constant stream that my overwhelmed mind can't seem to keep up with or concentrate on.

Half an hour, the coffee is cold, and my arms feel like jelly. Finally, Alexander wraps up the meeting, and the executives file out of the office.

I catch a few glances in my direction, no doubt noting my pitiable state: my shirt clinging to me with sweat, hair disheveled and damp against my skin—I must look like an absolute mess. A wave of embarrassment washes over me as they exit the office.

The room hangs in an oppressive silence as Alexander strides over, coming to a halt before me. In this position, his towering height makes me feel diminished, a sense of smallness enveloping me.

His piercing blue eyes seem to radiate an intensified brilliance as he glares down at me, and my hands instinctively clench the files I'm holding, bracing myself for what's to come.

"Give me one good reason why I shouldn't fire you right now," he murmurs, his hands buried deep in his pockets. I swallow hard, gaze dropping from his face to his impeccable shiny leather shoes. His grip tightens on my chin, forcing me to meet his gaze. "Look at me when I'm talking to you," he grumbles with a rough edge, his tongue momentarily moistening his lips.

Oh god, a wave of sensation courses through me at this side of Alexander, his eyes ablaze with anger. I secretly revel in the touch of his hands on my chin, an illicit thrill.

I subtly press my thighs together in my tight little skirt, feeling the heat rise. "I have no excuse. If you want to fire me, you should. I deserve it. I shouldn't have been so late for work. I'm truly sorry," I stammer, my words carrying a mix of regret and submission.

He remains silent, his gaze fixed upon me as if lost in contemplation. My breath quickens while my breasts hang heavily, pressing against the fabric of my chest. His warm breath grazes my face, and I can't help but notice the crimson hue of his lips; it's such an enticing sight. My heart clenches, resurfacing emotions I believed were long buried.

"Don't forget," he asserts, the words biting as his unwavering stare holds mine. "Being Abel's younger sister and my daughter's closest friend doesn't grant you special privileges.

I expect you to treat this job with the utmost respect and dedication," he states firmly. "Yes," I whisper breathlessly, catching a fleeting glimpse of an emotion in his eyes that vanishes as quickly as it appears.

"This is your first and final warning. Any further mistakes will result in termination. Do you understand?" he questions, his tone demanding.

I nod eagerly, and he gruffly adds, "Words, Olivia."

"Yes, sir," I respond, my voice obedient. He releases my chin, returning to his desk, leaving me quietly exhaling, already yearning for his comforting presence. "Fetch me another cup of coffee," he orders, his head bowed as he types on his computer.

"Yes, sir," I reply, hurrying out of the office, feeling slightly damp in my panties. I'm so screwed.

Chapter 4

Alexander

I have a strict policy against second chances. A mistake on the job meant one thing: you're out. Olivia, though, is different. Despite showing up late and appearing disheveled in my office, I hesitated to fire her, but something held me back.

At that moment, it was as if her green doe-like eyes held an unspoken plea, reaching out to me. I couldn't help but notice the subtle tension in her thick thighs, the contours defined by the snugness of her little skirt.

The rush of heat I felt when I sensed the weight of her breasts pressing firmly against my shirt. It was an undeniable magnetism, a pull that transcended the professional context. I found myself unable to cut ties; the decision to let her go suddenly became a task too heavy to bear.

A heavy sigh escapes as I rub my face, questioning my judgment. Her long-standing crush on me persisted when she and Abel left the country. Her eagerness to engage with me on calls and insistence on seeing me over video chats was all there.

I always brushed it off as a harmless crush that would fade over time. After all, we have a 20-year age gap, and she's my best friend's little sister. The mere thought of what Abel and Camila would think if they knew about my inappropriate reviews makes me shudder.

I need to focus on my work, I tell myself, attempting to block out these complicated feelings. Diving headfirst into my tasks might be the way to quell this surge of emotions.

"Thank you, Dante. Have a good night," I say, stepping out of the car. "You too, boss," he salutes.

Each step feels heavy as I make my way into the house, the gentle murmur of the water fountain in the compound providing a soothing backdrop. I place my palm on the door's hand sensor, which responds with a reassuring beep, granting me access. I kick off my shoes and casually drop my jacket over a nearby chair as I creep towards my bedroom.

"Oh God," I grunt, rolling my shoulders to relieve their tension. The thought of a massage feels like a distant dream right now.

After a much-needed and luxurious warm shower, I nestle into my bed, ready to embrace a night of rest, when suddenly, my phone rings. My eyes lock onto the name "Irene" on the screen. Why is she calling so late at night?

"What is it, Irene? Why are you calling so late?" I ask, my voice heavy with sleep and irritability.

"Uhm, I'm so sorry, but, but..." she stammers, her voice trembling slightly.

"Just spit it out," I urge, feeling my patience waning, my eyelids heavy.

"I forgot to tell you about the gala event you have tomorrow night," she rushes out in a single breath.

"What? I missed that. One word at a time, Irene," I sigh, pinching the bridge of my nose in frustration.

"I forgot to tell you about the gala event you have tomorrow night," she repeats more clearly.

"What gala event are you talking about?" I ask, incredulous. Irene is exceptional at her job; any crucial information should have been brought to my attention long before now. This isn't like her.

"It's the Matthew and Sons gala event, sir. It's happening tomorrow."

"Why are you just telling me now, and why didn't I know about this?" I can't help the irritation seeping into my voice. Anything involving Matthew and Sons is a necessary evil in our IT industry, and this gala event, despite my distaste for it, is the perfect platform to secure vital clients and present proposals to the industry's most influential CEOs.

"I'm so sorry, sir. I wanted to tell you today, but it completely slipped my mind," she apologizes.

"Is there anything going on at home?" I inquire, concerned. This oversight is unusual for Irene.

"Everything is fine, sir. I'm so sorry. Oh, and it's so sudden because the invitation arrived at the office this morning, right at my desk. I was supposed to give it to you personally," she explains timidly.

"It was a physical invite?" I clarify.

"Yes, sir."

Those .... They're purposely trying to mess with me. They've always emailed invitations, but now they've switched to physical invites; so much for being one of the leading IT companies in Chicago.

"Are you going to fire me, sir?" she asks, her voice trembling with worry over the phone.

"No," I say, a calm assurance in my voice.

"Oh, thank you so much, sir! This will never happen again," she responds with determination. If I granted Olivia a second chance, then Irene more than deserves one. She's been working for me for ten years and is excellent. Indeed, I can overlook this minor mistake.

"It is fine, Irene. We'll discuss this tomorrow. Goodnight," I conclude the call abruptly, realizing that extending second chances seems to be gradually becoming a recurring theme in my life.

"I'm sorry, what?" I've received this same bewildered reply for the past 20 minutes.

Olivia stands before me in my office, this time wearing a brown fitted dress that showcases her rich, creamy thighs, leaving little to the imagination. I can't help but notice how the dress clings to her curves, her body radiating an allure that could lead a man astray. I feel a stirring below, but I quickly shake my head to snap out. Focus, Alex.

"What part of what I said, don't you understand?" I ask, finding her reaction slightly amusing.

"I, I, I've never been to a gala event, sir," she spits, her eyes widening to their limits, her raised eyebrows nearly reaching her hairline.

Earlier this morning, after arriving at the office, Irene had shared a tiny yet critically important detail she'd omitted during her call last night. I needed a date for the gala event. Usually, I'd go by myself, defying their judgments.

But this time, Mr. Blake would be a top icon in the industry and a man known for his traditional views, who believes a man should have a woman by his side. I must make a lasting impression on him to secure one of my best deals.

Olivia wasn't my first l choice as a date for the gala event; I had other options. I could have hired an escort, but I needed someone I could easily guide, someone who'd carry themselves professionally, and in that aspect, Olivia seemed to be a perfect fit.

I'd encountered a few escorts before, but they often became overly intoxicated and flirtatious, causing embarrassing situations. However, with the sudden invitation to this event, Olivia seemed like the most reliable option. I was curious to see how she'd look in a dress.

"Well, you'll see," I mention casually as I read Daniel, my lawyer, text about an upcoming contract I must sign. "Go see Irene; she'll fill you in on all the details. See you at 7 pm sharp," I add, gesturing for her to go.

She nods, a puzzled expression lingering on her face. "And Olivia?" I inquire just as she's about to open the door handle. "Yes?" she responds, turning to face me. "Don't let me down," I assert, my tone conveying expectation.

"Are you sure this is a good idea?" Daniel's weary voice asks through the phone. "Unless you've got a better option, this is my best shot," I respond, kicking a random stone and pacing in front of Olivia's decrepit apartment building.

The poor structure looks like it's going to collapse anytime soon. I glance at my watch: 6:55 pm; I've stood here for twenty minutes.

"You know how brutal and sexist that gala can be, right? Is bringing Olivia wise? If Abel were here, he'd probably knock some sense into you," he remarks, a light chuckle accompanying his words.

"Olivia works with me now. She needs to understand our world and how to navigate it. I'll be there to support her, and let's leave Abel out of this," I reply, a hint of irritation in my voice, not keen on the implication that I can't protect her.

"No offense, but..." His words fade as I spot Olivia opening the door and descending the porch, a vision of elegance.

I had Irene choose a dress to complement my black suit, and it's a masterpiece. The black dress hugs her curves, accentuating her waist and revealing enough cleavage. Her lips, her pouty lips, are covered in a sultry shade of red to match her makeup, while her green eyes seem more vibrant than ever. She's stunning. I might have to give Irene a raise after this.

"Hi," she whispers, a subtle blush gracing her cheeks –endearing.

"You look stunning," I remark, reaching out my arms for her to place her hands into mine as we stroll towards my awaiting car.

Her gown frames her collarbones elegantly, and its graceful drape over her silhouette mesmerizes me. The fabric follows the contours of her body, revealing a hint of elegance and sensuality that's utterly irresistible.

"You clean up nicely, too," she teases with a smile.

The atmosphere is electric, with laughter, clinking glasses, and animated conversations echoing throughout the lavish venue. Various cliques occupy separate corners of the hall, discreetly aligning themselves by social status.

Their footwear, worth as much as a college education, glistens in the dim light while they exude an air of superiority, evident in their raised noses and confident posture. Everyone in this venue is impeccably dressed, flaunting their wealth, making it abundantly clear that this gala serves as a façade for the rich to show off their wealth.

"Alexander!" a voice, cherry yet raspy and one I detest, calls out to me. I summon a strained smile and pivot to face him, my hold on Olivia's back tightening discreetly. "Matthew, what a pleasure," I utter with forced charm, engaging in a handshake with him.

Matthew Moran's salt and pepper hair gleams beneath the chandelier, his dark eyes bearing a subtle, ominous glint. Despite being in his seventies, he's notorious for his questionable affairs with women much younger. The impunity he enjoys arises from his considerable influence.

"And who might this beauty be?" he inquires, a sly grin gracing his weathered face as he shifts his attention to Olivia. "This is my assistant, Olivia," I respond, my lips tightening as I introduce myself. Olivia courteously nods and greets him, "Nice to meet you, Sir." "Oh darling, call me Matthew," he insists, extending his hand, expecting Olivia to place hers within it.

I can sense Olivia's gaze on me from the corner of my eyes, and I give a subtle nod, my jaw clenched firmly. She extends her hand toward him, and he plants an unpleasantly wet, sloppy, and moist kiss on her hand. Afterward, Olivia discreetly wipes her hand on her dress. I experience a strange satisfaction knowing she doesn't like him either.

"Alexander, I'm afraid I need to speak with you," Matthew interjects, pausing briefly as he directs his gaze towards Olivia, "In private," he adds with a touch of urgency. "Are you going to be all right by yourself?"

I inquired, looking at Olivia, concern etched in my expression. "Yes," she replies, her assurance accompanied by a nod, "I'll be just fine."

"Are you sure?" I persist, reluctant to leave her alone in this unfamiliar, potentially hazardous environment, teeming with individuals concealed within their suits, who may not have the best intentions. "I'll be fine, Sir," she insists, a determined smile gracing her face. "We came here to secure a deal, right?

Go on, I'll be here, sipping on the ridiculously tasteful champagne". "Alex, when it's just me and you, call me Alex," I suggest. "Okay, Alex," a slight smile formed as her lips formed my name. It sounds enjoyable coming from her.

"All right," I turn back to Matthew, observing our brief exchange with a curious expression, "C'mon, let's go talk." The urgency of Matthew's request propels me, but I can't help but feel a pang of protective concern for Olivia as I follow Matthew to our private conversation.

After a grueling three-hour marathon of dull business discussions, I find myself behind the wheel with Olivia in the passenger seat, my decision to give Dante the day off leading to a solo drive today.

"So, how was it?" I inquired, glancing at Olivia while deftly maneuvering onto the next street. "Boring," she declares. Unexpectedly, hearty laughter escapes my lips; it's a departure from the usual scripted responses I encounter from the escorts I accompany to these gala events.

Most of them plaster on a fake smile and claim it was fun, so encountering someone who genuinely didn't enjoy it is refreshing.

My laughter recedes as Olivia speaks, her tone laced with curiosity. "Did I say something funny?" she inquires. "No, not really. It's just refreshing to meet someone who isn't fond of those gala events," I respond. "Why do you go to them then?" she probes.

A deep exhale escapes my lips, and I pause momentarily before answering, "Let's just say It's a necessary evil," I confess, pulling up to her apartment building.

"Thank you for tonight, Olivia," I express, as genuinely as possible, turning in my seat to face her. "My pleasure, Alex," she responds. Our gaze remains locked, granting me a view of the rich hues of brown beneath the vibrant green of her eyes. I notice a small mole just above her right eyebrow.

My gaze instinctively lowers to her lips, an irresistible allure that has held my attention throughout the evening. Her tongue swipes out and brushes over her bottom lip, and the sight triggers an involuntary groan that escapes my lips. "Uhm, I have to go now," she murmurs breathlessly.

"Yeah, sure," I respond, mentally berating myself. "Goodnight, Olivia." "Night, Alex," she softly replies. As I drive home, a noticeable bulge in my pants reminds me of our intense attraction.

Chapter 5

Olivia

"So, how was it?" Irene's eager eyes lock onto me from the cubicle. A smile forms on my lips as I gather some documents for Alex. "Boring," I respond, a casual tone accompanying my words.

"Boring!" Irene exclaims, her hands gripping the top of the cubicle, her eyes widening in disbelief. I merely shrug my shoulders, a nonchalant gesture that doesn't lessen her surprise.

A wistful sigh escapes her lips as she leans against the cubicle wall, a dreamy look on her face.

"Wow, I had always yearned to attend that gala," she murmurs. Her gaze shifts back to me, a playful glint in her eye as she continues, "I hoped you might have found some enjoyment there, so I could at least live vicariously through you. Oh Lord," she adds, rolling her eyes in mock exasperation.

In the weeks that have passed, Irene and I have grown close. I discovered that she is a single mother whose husband ran off with her nanny, the horror. Despite her challenges, her love for her six-year-old son, Benjamin, shines through.

She once said she implored Alexander to grant her a job opportunity, even without the requisite qualifications. Her gratitude for his kindness and belief in her resonates deeply, especially after numerous rejections from other companies due to her status as a single mother.

But those companies' loss is undoubtedly our gain. Irene has proven to be one of the most exceptional employees I've ever encountered; her presence here is well-deserved and invaluable.

Just then, a group of men dressed in impeccably tailored suits strides past us, each holding a briefcase cradled in their arms. I cast a sidelong glance at Irene, my curiosity getting the better of me. "Who are they?" I inquire in a hushed tone.

With a knowing smile, Irene leans conspiratorially, her voice barely audible as she divulges, "Oh, those are Mr. McQueen's guests. They come around once a month." Her tone hints at a mysterious air as she continues, "It's pretty secretive; no one is permitted to enter their gathering.

Frankly, I'm clueless about their activities behind those doors. But without fail, after their meeting concludes, we're handed this massive deal that demands our attention."

A bemused shake of her head accompanies her following words as she leans in closer, her terms a confidential whisper, "We're always swamped with work following their meeting, but I must admit, there's a silver lining. We're generously rewarded with substantial bonuses on our paychecks."

Curiously, I raise an eyebrow, finding the situation rather peculiar. "But what about these documents?" I motion toward the files neatly arranged on the desk.

"Alex, err, sorry, Mr. McQueen had urgently requested these," I explain, a silent hope lingering within me that Irene doesn't pick up on my familiarity in addressing him by his name.

It felt like a more intimate gesture, a bond I wanted to keep between us. Perhaps I only imagine it, and he suggested using his first name solely due to our friendship, yet the notion elicits a private smile.

Her response carries a hint of mischief as she speaks, "Oh, just wait until they're finished, though it might take quite a while. Sometimes, I can't help but wonder if they're up to something in there." A sly smirk graces her lips as she adds a layer of intrigue to her words.

Perplexed, I furrow my brows, genuinely unaware of her implication. "What do you mean?" I inquire, my curiosity piqued.

In a calm tone, Irene leans in again, her lips close to my ear, her words laden with the suggestion, "Oh, darling, I've often speculated whether they might be engaging in some... intimate activities."

Taken aback by her audacious statement, I released a startled exclamation, "Oh God, Irene!" My outburst earns me a few curious glances from our colleagues nearby.

Unfazed by my reaction, she nonchalantly shrugs, whispering, "It's entirely plausible." A playful smile spreads across her lips, leaving me momentarily speechless.

Chapter 6

Alexander

The insistent ring of my phone cuts through the quiet of my apartment, and I nearly drop my book in surprise. The caller ID flashes "Abel," and my heart skips a beat. It's been three years of radio silence from his end.

I had tried reaching out to him in many ways—text messages, emails, hell. I even wanted to fly across the city to see him, but I didn't know where he was exactly. The last time I checked, he was in Brazil, but I do not know where he is now.

I tried contacting Olivia, but my attempts had been met with the same frustrating silence. She, too, had become unreachable as Abel, leaving me with no way to gain insight into their lives or whereabouts. I had intended to ask Olivia about her brother's location once she began working for me.

It seemed the perfect opportunity to glean information without me prying too much. But as I observed Olivia, it became apparent that she was doing well, seemingly unaffected by the distance from her brother. She appeared composed, not displaying any signs of worry or apprehension, so I assumed he was doing okay and was just in those moods or phases where he just wanted to be alone.

After that incident several years back, when he left, we kept in touch despite our busy schedules.

So, when he went off the grid, I was worried, thinking something terrible had happened. My worry turned to relief when, out of the blue, a text from him arrived, a terse message saying, "I'm fine, don't look for me." It was quintessentially "Abel-like"—straightforward and persistent, yet devoid of insight into his thoughts or feelings. It was one of the few things I hated about him.

Picking up the phone with no hesitation,
Hey, Abel? Is that you?" I manage to say, my voice betraying surprise and cautious excitement.

There's a brief pause, a hesitation that makes my pulse quicken. "Alex? Yeah, it's me," comes Abel's voice, a little weary yet unmistakably him.

"Where the hell have you been, man?" I was worried about you," I say as I make coffee in the kitchen.

"I'm sorry, Alex, but I, you know, needed, uhm... time for myself, "he sighs as he says over the phone.

Relief courses through my veins; I'm happy he's fine, yet I resent him. It's been three years- three long years of silence.

I at least thought he would have reached out to me, even if once. Abel is my best friend and has been my best friend ever since I saved him from getting his ass bullied in kindergarten; we practically grew up together, so it's annoying that he just decided to go off without telling me.

"That's fine, so how're you doing now?" I ask carefully. Dancing around the topic, I probe, "How's therapy?" It has always been a sensitive topic around Abel, but I need to know if he's doing all right and hasn't returned to taking drugs to give him some fake euphoria.

"Where the hell have you been, man?" I exclaim, unable to contain the relief and frustration bubbling beneath the surface. I pace around the kitchen, my agitation evident as I reach for the coffee supplies. My heart is still pounding from the shock of hearing his voice after three years of silence.

"I'm sorry, Alex, but I just... You know, needed, uh, time for myself," he replies with a heavy sigh, his voice a mix of exhaustion and hesitation.

As I prepare the coffee, I take a deep breath, trying to calm my swirling emotions—relief courses through my veins like a soothing balm. I'm glad that he's okay and that he's at least reached out now. But alongside that relief, there's an undeniable undercurrent of resentment.

Three years—three long years of nothingness. I had been worried sick, imagining the worst scenarios. I had hoped that he would have reached out, even just once. After all, Abel isn't just any friend; he's been my best friend since kindergarten, ever since I stood up to bullies who thought it was fun to target him. We've practically grown up together, and it's beyond annoying that he decided to disappear without so much as a word.

"That's fine," I reply, my voice tense but trying to temper my emotions. I can't help but roll my eyes at his vague explanation. "So, how're you doing now?"

His response is quiet, a pause that stretches between us like an unspoken understanding. "I'm... I'm getting there. It's been a journey, Alex. Therapy's been helping, slowly."

I nod, even though he can't see me, and I'm grateful that he's willing to share even this much. Therapy has always been a sensitive topic around Abel, a subject he would deflect or avoid.

My heart sinks at the reminder of that fateful day that changed our lives forever. I had witnessed firsthand how deeply it had affected Abel, and I respect his need to heal on his terms.

However, I want to know that he's progressing and not reverting to the self-destructive tendencies he struggled with. I need the reassurance that he's finding healthier ways to cope.

"Good, I'm glad to hear that," I say, trying to keep my voice steady and supportive. "Just remember, I'm here for you, Abel, no matter what. You could've told me what you were going through. I thought we shared everything."

There's a moment of silence on the other end of the line, and I can almost picture him running a hand through his hair, a habit he always had when he was nervous. "I know, Alex. And I'm sorry. I should've reached out, but... it was complicated."

I sighed, and the tension in my shoulders eased a fraction. "Look, I get that. We all have our battles to fight, and I respect that. But I'm just glad you're back. You scared the crap out of me, you know?"

He chuckles like a lifeline, reminding me of our familiar camaraderie. "Yeah, I figured I would. Sorry about that."

As our conversation unfolds, it's almost as if time rewinds itself. We pick up where we left off, like a well-worn book with pages that have been thumbed through countless times. We discuss the minutiae of our lives—the new deals my company has, the book he's currently engrossed in, and how I'm this close to firing the cleaner.

That woman sleeps on the job, and I'm not exaggerating; she sleeps anywhere, at any time.

And then, amid our conversation, comes the inevitable question. "So, how's Olivia doing? I hear she's working for you now."

I pause for a moment, wanting to sound as natural as possible. "Oh, she's doing great; she's dedicated to her job. You trained her well, Abel".

There's a moment of silence for a while.

"I must confess, I find that quite surprising," Abel finally responds with a mixture of curiosity and something much more challenging to decipher. "I had no idea she was even considering working for you."

"Yeah, it kind of took me by surprise, too," I admit, my heart racing slightly.

"I'm happy she chose to work with you, Alex," Abel continues, his words carrying a sincerity that's hard to ignore. "She couldn't have found a better place or person to work with, and I trust you'll take good care of her."

I feel a heavy pang of guilt settle in the pit of my stomach, an overwhelming wave of shame crashing over me. Abel's trust in me is unwavering, yet he remains oblivious to my secret turmoil. He places his sister in my care, believing she's safe with me, not knowing the twisted thoughts that have begun to gnaw at my conscience.

It's a torment that I can't escape, a sickening realization of the desires that have taken root in my mind. I watch Olivia, the girl I've known since she was a kid, the same girl who has become an intricate part of our lives. But now, my perception has warped, my thoughts have darkened, and it's all I can do to resist the sinister pull that beckons me toward the edge of an abyss.

Every encounter is a battle to suppress the hard-on that threatens to betray me. It's a constant fight to mask my escalating attraction, hide how my gaze lingers just a fraction too long, and conceal the rush of blood that surges to my groin whenever she's near. The shame is a heavy burden, a stain on my bond with Abel, forged in friendship and trust.

My nights have become a battleground of their own. Alone in the shower after a long day's work, my mind conjures seductive and depraved images. The creamy softness of her thighs, the curve of her ass, and the contours of her body that I've been fighting to ignore invade my thoughts like a relentless storm. It's a battle of morality and desire, a clash that leaves me feeling tainted and disgusted with myself.

I try to resist fisting my rigid member in my shower every night when I return from work. As the water pours over me, I close my eyes and try to quell the fantasies that threaten to engulf me. I try to focus on anything else, on trivialities, on mundane thoughts that might chase away the darkness that looms. But it's a futile struggle, a fight tearing me from the inside out.

My mind involuntarily goes to that fateful incident in my office last week. It's a memory that taunts me, a reminder of my weakness, and a testament to the boundary I've dared to tread. The image of her walking in, filling the room with intoxicating energy, is etched into my mind. I can practically feel the weight of that moment, like a heavy secret I'm forced to carry.

My heart races as I recall the simple offering of cake—an innocent gesture that ignited a fire I couldn't seem to extinguish. The memory plays out in slow motion, her hand extending, the plate of cake balanced precariously, and the subtle twitch of her lips as she meets my gaze. But it's her eyes; those damned eyes betrayed a hunger I had never seen before— a hunger that mirrored my desires, desires I knew were forbidden, dangerous.

As I accepted the cake from her hand, the air between us crackled with an electric arc of tension. The softness of her fingers against my skin sent a jolt of sensation straight to the pit of my stomach, a feeling I couldn't ignore. I remember her breath catching, a barely audible hitch that spoke volumes. It was a moment that hung suspended in time, a threshold I was about to cross, a line I was perilously close to obliterating.

And then, that image—the one that torments me most—flashes before my eyes. The moment I brought her fingers to my lips, the taste of sweetness mingled with the heady anticipation that hummed in the air. Her eyes held mine captive, dark pools of desire that threatened to pull me under. I can practically feel the clench of her thighs, the subtle arch of her back, the way her body seemed to react to my touch.

The mere thought of it sends a jolt through me, my body betraying me in the most primal ways. I shift uncomfortably in my seat, the fabric of my pants now an unwelcome restraint. I shake my head forcefully, trying to banish the images that have become an unwanted obsession.

The guilt I feel every day is a bitter taste that coats every word, every gesture, and every interaction. I force myself to smile around Olivia, to maintain the facade of a friend, a protector. But underneath it all, I'm battling the urges that threaten to consume me, the desires that have twisted my perspective beyond recognition.

"Yeah," I reply, the words punctuated by the lukewarm coffee in my cup. I take a sip, hoping to appear composed despite the turmoil that simmers beneath the surface. "I'm glad I accepted her too. She's turned out to be an invaluable asset to my company."

"Yeah, I want—" Abel's voice cuts off abruptly, replaced by a flurry of muffled sounds I can barely decipher. "Yo! We got to go!" someone shouts in the background, followed by a hurried exchange of voices.

"Hey, I have to go now," Abel's words are rushed, urgency lacing his tone as he speaks into the phone's speaker. "It was nice talking to you, Alex," he says before the connection is severed.

The line goes dead, leaving me staring at my phone, a heaviness settling in my chest. I set the coffee cup down with a sigh, the remnants of our conversation still hanging like unspoken truths.

Frustration bubbles up within me as I run my hands roughly over my face. "Alex, what the hell is wrong with you?" I mutter to myself, my voice tinged with disbelief and self-disgust. I'm acting like a damn teenager, all giddy and uncertain. It starkly contrasts the composed, successful businessman I've become.

I take a moment to remind myself of who I am, to ground myself in reality. At 43 years old, I've built a thriving company from the ground up. I've faced challenges, made tough decisions, and earned the respect of my peers. I've got a beautiful daughter who looks up to me, who would be devastated and disappointed if she ever found out about the mess of feelings I've allowed to fester.

With a heavy exhale, I shake my head, determined to regain control over my emotions. I can't afford to let this infatuation unravel the life I've built. I'm not the impulsive fool I seem to have become. I need to get my priorities straight to focus on what truly matters—the well-being of my company, the happiness of my daughter, and the integrity of the friendships I hold dear.

Olivia is off limits, I remind myself with a fierce determination, the words like a mantra I need to repeat until they're etched into my memory. I can't afford to let this desire consume me, to let it tear down the walls I've built over years of friendship and trust. It's a struggle, a battle against the darkness that's clawing at the edges of my restraint.

But I can't let it win. The stakes are too high, the consequences too dire. Olivia deserves better than the twisted thoughts that have taken residence in my mind. Abel's trust and our history deserve more than the betrayal that simmers beneath the surface.

So, I grit my teeth, pushing away the memories that threaten to overwhelm me, forcing my focus elsewhere. I have to remind myself, again and again, that Olivia is not an object of my fantasies. She's a person—Abel's sister, my daughter's best friend —and she deserves my respect, restraint, and unwavering commitment to keeping those boundaries intact.

Chapter 7

O *livia*

"Hey, can I talk to you for a bit?" Richard's voice breaks through the hum of the office, and I glance up from my computer to find him standing in front of my cubicle.

His tousled brown hair falls gracefully, nearly obscuring his eyeglasses, and the brown cashmere sweater he's wearing brings out the warmth in his light brown eyes. A pair of black slacks and polished loafers complete his attire, making him look effortlessly put together.

"Yeah, sure," I reply in a hushed tone, mindful not to disrupt the workflow around us. With a slight nod, I rise from my seat, and Richard steps aside to let me pass. He steps beside me as we navigate the maze of cubicles and walk to the break room.

Once inside, the room feels oddly empty and quiet compared to the bustling office beyond its walls. The soft hum of the vending machines and the distant chatter from the open office layout create a subtle background ambiance.

Richard turns to me, his gaze sincere as he clears his throat. "I've been meaning to talk to you about something," he begins, his voice steady yet tinged with nervousness.

I lean against the edge of a table, folding my arms loosely. "Sure, what's on your mind?" I ask, genuinely interested to hear what he has to say.

He takes a moment to gather his thoughts, his fingers absentmindedly tracing the rim of his coffee cup. "I wanted to ask if you'd like to grab coffee with me sometime outside work."

His question catches me off guard, and for a moment, I'm lost in his light brown eyes, searching for any hint of his intentions. There's something vulnerable in his gaze, as if he's laying a part of himself bare for me to see.

"Coffee?" I repeat, my voice softening. "Like a...date?"

A shy smile tugs at the corners of his lips, and he nods. "Yeah, exactly. If you're interested, that is."

I hesitate, uncertainty swirling in my thoughts like leaves caught in a gentle breeze. "Uhmm... I'm not sure..." I begin, my voice trailing off as I search for the right words to convey my feelings.

But before I finish my sentence, Richard's voice cuts through the air, urgent and determined. "Wait!" he interjects, raising his hand as if to halt my words physically. His eyes hold a mixture of earnestness and vulnerability, a glimpse into the depth of his emotions.

"Before you shut me down or refuse the offer, I want you to know something," he continues, his words carefully chosen and delivered with undeniable sincerity.

He pauses momentarily, collecting his thoughts and locking eyes with me as if trying to bridge the gap between us. "I like you. I've liked you ever since I saw you walk through that door," he admits, his voice carrying a quiet intensity. "And I would like it if you could agree to go on this date with me, just this once. Give us a chance to see where things could go."

His words hang in the air like a delicate web spun between us. I feel a mixture of surprise and curiosity, his honesty catching me off guard. I've known Richard as a coworker, someone I exchange occasional conversations with by the coffee machine, but I hadn't anticipated the depth of his feelings.

"And if you don't like it," he adds, a hint of vulnerability in his tone, "I promise I won't ever bother you again."

I gaze at Richard, my mind racing as I consider his words. "Okay," I shrug and say, my voice carrying a mix of hesitation and acquiescence.

"Okay," he exclaims, his eyes lighting up with surprise and delight. A short burst of laughter escapes his lips, a nervous but genuine response to my unexpected agreement.

If I agree to this, I'll be able to let him down and gently nudge away any budding romantic feelings he might be harboring for me. Richard is a great guy, but I know deep down that I need this to end on a clean slate.

"Yeah," I say, a small smile forming as I meet Richard's gaze.

"Wow, that's amazing," he says, his tone light but genuine. "How about tonight? Could we check out that cinema hall that opened downtown and see a movie?" Richard suggests with excitement, his eyes lighting up as he presents the idea.

"Sounds like a plan," I reply, wondering what I have just gotten myself into.

"What do you wear to a cinema with a date?" I ask, holding the phone against my ear and steadying it with my shoulder, my free hand rummaging through my closet.

"You're going on a date?" Camila's voice erupts from the phone, an explosive burst of excitement that catches me off guard. I wince slightly at how loud she is, muttering a quiet "Jesus" as I cradle the phone between my ear and shoulder.

"Who is he? Where did you meet him? How handsome is he? Oooh... have you guys kissed? Or maybe even had sex? I don't know,

I don't judge, I need all the details!" Camila's words tumble out in a frantic rush; her enthusiasm is palpable even through the phone's receiver. Oh Lord, she's relentless.

I roll my eyes, a fond exasperation tugging at the corners of my lips as I respond, "He's a coworker, his name is Richard. No, we haven't kissed yet, and we haven't had sex. For God's sake, Camila, this is our first date," I sigh, momentarily flustered by her barrage of questions. I collect myself and continue, "He's handsome." I pause for a beat, a smirk playing at my lips before adding, "In the nerdish way."

"Oooh... Richard," she teases playfully, her voice infused with a mischievous lilt. "With those slacks he's usually wearing and those brown eyes that seem to stare endlessly into your soul, oh, I understand why you're going on a date with him," she adds, her words accompanied by a dreamy sigh that carries through the phone line.

"Okay, okay, we get it, he makes your panties wet, period," I chuckle in response, my tone light as I toss a few dresses onto my bed, scanning through them for the right choice. The phone now rests comfortably in my hands, allowing me to continue our conversation.

"Oh no, I'm more into, you know, the one who gives me 'daddy' vibes," she remarks, her voice taking on a playful edge. "No offense, but Richard doesn't look like one who'd be into those types of kinky shit."

Camila's candidness never fails to amuse me, and I can't help but laugh at her boldness. "Well, not everyone has to fit into your 'daddy' category," I retort, my smile evident. "But trust me, Richard has his charm now. Will you please help me pick a dress?"

I selected a delicate pale pink halter dress from the jumble of slacks, sweatshirts, and t-shirts in my closet, which I could credit mostly to Camila's input. It was, after all, the most decent option I could find at that moment. Damn, I need to shop for more dresses.

I arrive at the cinema a little late, and my eyes scan the area, searching for any sign of Richard amidst the bustling crowd.

The cinema lobby is a realm of vibrant anticipation. Its walls are adorned with larger-than-life posters, each one showcasing the latest blockbusters in vivid colors and compelling scenes. The air carries a heady scent of buttered popcorn and sweet confections from the candy counter, a sensory reminder of the movie magic that awaits inside.

The muted lighting casts a warm glow over the space, a deliberate invitation to leave the mundane world behind and step into the world of imagination. Conversations buzz like a symphony of whispers, punctuated by the occasional burst of laughter or the hum of excitement.

I spot a couple nearby – a young girl seated on a low counter, her legs dangling slightly above the ground. I assume her boyfriend crouches in front of her, his fingers deftly tending to fix her shoelaces. A tender smile forms on her lips as she gazes down at him, her cheeks tinged with a delicate blush that paints her face with warmth and affection. A deep sigh escapes my lips, carrying a tinge of longing as I watch the couple. I can't help but wonder when I'll experience that same kind of connection when I can gaze at someone with such genuine affection and tenderness.

A sudden tap on my shoulder startles me, causing me to whirl around to face the source of the interruption. It's Richard, standing before me with a faint smile. "I'm sorry if I scared you," he says, his voice carrying a note of concern. His brown hair is neatly slicked back, and he's abandoned his glasses in favor of contacts, his eyes appearing even more captivating than before. He's dressed impeccably in a black jacket, a crisp white shirt underneath, and black jeans and sneakers.

A sudden wave of self-consciousness washes over me as I glance down at my pale pink halter dress and heels. Suddenly, I feel a tad overdressed amidst his casually cool ensemble.

"You look beautiful tonight," he compliments, his gaze sweeping over me. "You look nice, too," I respond with a smile. "Come on, let's head inside; the movie's about to start," he urges, guiding me toward the entrance.

Getting into his car, we start talking about the movie we watched. Amidst fits of laughter, I exclaim, "That was so funny!" My chest heaves joyfully, and I absentmindedly reach for the remaining popcorn. "Absolutely," Richard chimes in, his face illuminated by amusement. "The cliff-jumping scene had me in stitches."

As we approach a nearby bus stop, I say, "You can stop here." He says, "You don't have to get off here; I can drive you home." I decline, explaining, "No worries, just drop me off here. My house is out of your way."

He pulls over, the engine quiets, and silence lingers. Breaking it, I express, "Thank you for tonight; it' was enjoyable." "Yeah, it is," he agrees, his brown eyes fixed on me. Drawing closer, his face almost touching mine, he hesitates. I lean back, murmuring, "I don't think that's a good idea."

Understanding, he settles back into his seat. "Oh," he acknowledges softly. Wanting to clarify, I turn towards him, saying, "Richard, you're a fantastic friend. While tonight was wonderful, I don't sense a deeper connection between us. I think we're better off as friends."

"It's cool; I'm just glad I got to do this with you," he says. "Yeah, bye," I say as I exit the car.

He waves at me from inside his car, and I wave back, and then he zooms off.

I hail the next taxi and take a ride home.

Upon exiting the taxi, I head to my apartment building. My footsteps resonate with a clicking sound. My feet are killing me; I can't wait to take off these heels. Unexpectedly, a voice emerges from behind, inquiring, "How come I don't see you around anymore?" I pivot to find Michael, his basketball in hand, as always

Sighing, I lean on one of my legs and say, "What are you doing here, Michael? Are you stalking me?" I tease. Snorting, he says, "Oh, don't flatter yourself; I'm waiting for someone." he nods, gesturing towards my building.

It is then that I notice his unusual attire: a suit. A laugh escapes me, prompting a question about his formal attire. "Why are you wearing a suit?" I ask incredulously. "Why are you wearing a suit?" His lips curl up in a smile, "I look good, don't I?" He asks cockily. "Uhm... no," I say, shaking my head.

That's a lie; he looks nice, has a haircut, is clean-shaven, and even has on these sparkling clean shoes, but I would not tell him all these; his ego is big enough already.

"Touché," he says, bouncing the ball forward and hitting my chest with it, "Hey!" I protest, to which he counters by sticking out his tongue. Yeah, typical Michael.

"Well, happy waiting," I quip, entering the building. Just then, a lady walks out the door, dressed in short shorts and a tube top, legs in sneakers, and her blonde hair a fried mess. "Hey, babe!" She says.

"Babe"? I mutter, turning my head to see her rush into Michael's embrace. He lifts her off the ground, tenderly contrasting his usual demeanor. Their gentle exchange leaves me chuckling incredulously; that's interesting.

Chapter 8

Alexander

The office air feels stagnant as I glance across the room and catch a glimpse of them, Olivia and Richard, huddled together in quiet conversation. A pang of unease twists in my gut. The searing heat of jealousy courses through me, a molten river of anger and confusion that I struggle to contain.

I never thought I'd feel this way – me, Alexander, the guy who's always had his emotions in check. But seeing her with him, so cozy and comfortable, ignites something in me that I can't easily brush off.

Yesterday, as I made my way to the break room to make coffee and get some biscuits, the sounds of people conversing from the closed door brought my steps to a halt.

It seemed like a private conversation. My employees had the habit of having private discussions in the break room. Ordinarily, I wouldn't have lingered by the door, but the unmistakable sound of Olivia's voice held me captive. He had asked her on a date, and she agreed. I remember my hands tightly gripping the door's handle; it took all I had not to barge into the room.

I take it their date went well, seeing as they're huddled up together, whispering and giggling, the way her laughter dances through the air, as they chat like old friends. Old friends. That's how she's acting with him, while we've known each other for most of our lives. A bitter taste lingers in my mouth, juxtaposed with the unintended snap of my pen-gripped hand, which serves as a jarring reminder of reality. An involuntary expletive punctuates my thoughts – "shit!"

I press the intercom button on the desk, now linked to her work-space, "Get in here, Irene," I say. I watch as she mutters something to Richard, who nods his head, then she stands up and starts walking down to my office; I notice Richard's lingering gaze on her round ass; if only he weren't my employee.....

As I sit there, I find myself crafting excuses – reasons to dismiss the rising feelings within me. I try to convince myself that it's not about jealousy but her professionalism or lack thereof. Maybe she's too casual, too carefree. That's why she can let her guard down and bond with someone like Richard. He's not her superior, not someone she has to impress.

When Olivia walks in, I greet her with a curt nod, making sure to keep my expression distant.

"I need you to arrange those files over there." I point towards the disordered pile of weighty files at the far corner of my office desk. "Alphabetically," I add.

"Uhm... do I have to finish all of these today?" She asks, her gaze on me. "Yes", I reply curtly.

"Okay....." she says, raising an eyebrow, probably sensing the shift in my demeanor, but she doesn't say anything else. He nods and gets to work.

I watch her from the corner of my eye as she sorts the documents aside. But I can't help myself; I want her to feel what I'm feeling, even though I'm not entirely sure what that is. It's like I'm torn between wanting to protect her and wanting to push her away – and I can't decipher which impulse is more vital.

The day stretches on, the tension between us growing palpable. I find myself snapping at her for minor mistakes, criticizing her for things that aren't her fault. It's unlike me – I've always been composed and level-headed. But now, every interaction with her stokes the fire of frustration that's been simmering beneath the surface.

When she finally finishes my assigned tasks, I don't give up. I give her more work, barely concealing my irritation. She must be wondering what's gotten into me. But I can't seem to stop myself; it's like a force beyond my control is propelling me forward.

"Is there anything else?" she inquires, her voice carrying a trace of weariness. It's evening, leaving the office sparsely occupied while the moonlight's delicate beams softly weave a faint shadow across the room.

"Nothing else; you can leave now," I said coldly. She nods and is about to leave the office when she stops, turns to me, her expression a mix of confusion, and says, "Did I do anything wrong?" Her voice is tinged with a hint of hurt and cuts through me like a knife.

I feel a rush of guilt for the way I've treated her. Maybe my frustration wasn't entirely about her. Perhaps it was about my inability to process what's happening within me, but despite that, the fact that whatever I'm feeling right now is morally wrong is at the forefront of my mind.

I harden my countenance and retort, "I was unaware that carrying out your responsibilities had become 'something wrong.' You are free to leave Olivia."

"Sure," she mumbles softly, her departure accompanied by the muted click of her heels.

"Damn!" I mutter under my breath, exasperating, running my hands across my face.

Chapter 9

Olivia

Over the past few days, I've been on the receiving end of Alex's sour disposition. Without apparent cause, he's directed his anger toward me and assigned menial tasks to me. I swear he's trying to punish me for something. I rack my head through the mental list of things he's given me to do for the past week, and I have done every damned thing, so I have no clue why he's treating me this way.

"You look like a wreck," Irene's voice remarks as she stands before me. "Gee, thanks, just the right words I needed to hear today," I retort sarcastically.

"I've heard about what's been happening. Are you certain you didn't unintentionally provoke him?" She whispers, her large eyes locked onto mine.

Curious, I ask in a hushed tone, "How did you know about that?" "The walls have ears, my dear," she quips. A deep sigh escapes me as I slump into my seat. "I genuinely don't recall doing anything to upset him," I respond.

"Could it be his usual mood swings?" I wonder, my shoulders lifting in a nonchalant shrug as I glance up at Irene. Drawing closer, she leans in and says, "Look, I've been around here for quite a while, and I've never witnessed our boss in such a pissy mood. You sure nothing happened?"

"I was just about to explode—" I start to reply, but I'm abruptly interrupted by the buzzing of the intercom on my desk. Alex's voice pierces through, "I need you in my office." With a resigned sigh, I rise from my seat and head toward his office, glancing at Irene, who silently mouths, "Good luck."

With a deep breath, curiosity gnawing at me, I grasp the door handle and step inside. Alex stands at the edge of the expansive conference table, his hips casually leaning against it while he goes through some documents on the table. "You called for me?" I inquire. He turns, his gaze a blank stare. "Yeah, come over here," he waves me over.

I approach with composed steps, stopping by his side. His finger indicates the computer before us. "What do you think about this proposal?" he asks. Leaning in, I catch a hint of his spicy, cinnamon scent; God, he smells so good. "It's impressive," I remark. "The priorities are well-structured, projecting confidence without any sign of desperation. Given the advantageous terms for them, they're likely to accept."

"All right, you're dismissed," he replies, clicking his computer. "That's all?" I query if this was the sole reason for my presence. A lift of his eyebrow accompanies his response. "Indeed. Unless, of course, you have any other plans for me?"

I chuckle softly. "No," I reply. "There's nothing. Excuse me then." With that, I exit his office.

"At least he didn't kill you," Irene quips, her figure perched at my desk. "Yet," she adds with a teasing grin. I roll my eyes playfully, retorting, "Don't you have work to do?"

"Well, had you glanced at the clock, you'd have realized it is lunchtime," she scolds. Only then do I notice that the office is relatively empty. Glancing at my phone, I remark, "Wow, time completely escaped me."

"Naturally, that's why I'm here to rescue you, honey," she chuckles while lifting me. "You're having lunch with me."

The door makes a ding sound as we walk in. A welcoming aroma embraces me—a medley of aromatic spices and sizzling ingredients. The cozy dining area is adorned with a mix of wooden and metal furnishings, radiating a casual and inviting vibe. At the same time, Soft ambient lighting illuminates the space, creating a relaxed atmosphere.

I've been here a couple of times, but this is my first time with someone else - Irene. After placing our order, we reached a snug table at the back.

"So, what's your story?" Irene's question slices through the air. I glance at the drink menu, my eyes catching the unexpected inclusion of 'sex on the beach'—when did they slip that onto the list?

"What do you mean?" I deflect, my fingers skimming the menu's pages. A smirk dances on her lips, hands raised in mock surrender. "Your relationship with Mr. McQueen," she clarifies. "I don't mean any offense, but after checking your file, you're overqualified for a personal assistant role. So, why take it?" Her gaze locks onto mine, brimming with intensity.

As if on cue, the waiter places our steaming dishes before us. "Thank you," we both chime in unison. "Olivia?" Irene calls me back, her tone gentle. "I won't pry if you'd rather not share. We're getting closer, and I realize I know nearly nothing about you."

Heavy with the weight of the past I've meticulously tucked away, a sigh escapes me. My history is a jar of secrets, a treasure chest buried in the depths of the sea. Yet, talking to someone could provide a sliver of relief.

"I have an older brother, Abel. He's twenty years older than me and my favorite person. We went through something callous together. We lost our parents in a fire when I was just four years old—" I pause, gathering the strength to continue.

"Uh, one evening, he had some friends over from his college days, just a casual gathering. Our parents were okay with it, and they headed to their rooms, letting the young ones have their fun as long as it was kept down. I recall asking Abel if I could stay and join them, and he agreed. You know, at that moment, he was my hero, the epitome of cool," a gentle chuckle escapes me as I reminisce, accompanied by a sip o f water.

Irene's compassionate eyes rest on me as she reassures me, "You don't have to continue if it's too painful."

Gathering my thoughts, I press on. "Abel and his friends got carried away, got a bit drunk, and decided to whip up some soup in the kitchen. When the gathering ended, his friends left, and he carried me upstairs, tucking me into bed. A loud, abrupt awakening came next, with my mom's panic-stricken voice. She thrust me into Abel's arms and told him to get me out of the house—little did I know it was the last time I'd see our parents alive.

The following memories are a bit blurry, but I remember Abel blaming himself. He left the gas on, which ultimately ignited the fire. Our parents made the ultimate sacrifice to get us out. We barely escaped before the house erupted into flames. When firefighters arrived, the house was reduced to ashes; our parents lost inside."

Across the table, Irene reaches out, her hand gently over mine. Her presence is comforting as the weight of that tragic memory washes over me.

"Abel was deeply affected by what happened, and we had to move out of the country; staying in Chicago was a harsh reminder. Alex and Camila were the ones who were there for us; they stuck with us through thick and thin. They even tried to convince Abel not to go; they wanted to help, but you know, men and their ridiculous egos.

Abel didn't want anything from them, so we had to leave, went to Brazil, and started over. It wasn't easy; sometimes, we didn't get to eat three square meals a day, but Abel made sure I didn't go to bed hungry, even if he had to sacrifice himself. I came back to Chicago at 18. I wanted to return and leave Brazil, but Abel wasn't ready, so I came alone. Of course, Camila found me immediately when I landed in Chicago", and I let out a breathy laugh as I recounted the memory.

"I continued my education here, all thanks to Camila and Alex, of course, and here I am, working here, a hell of a story, right?" My lips form a bittersweet smile

Irene's words pull me from the memories, her slight smile comforting me. "I'm grateful you shared this with me," she murmurs. "You've faced so much, but things will be better from now on, hmm?"

I give a half-hearted nod. "Yeah, yeah," I reply. "Come on; our food is getting cold; let's eat."

"Nooo... that's wild!" I exclaim with a chuckle, my disbelief evident in my tone. "I was surprised myself! You should have seen me – I was too shocked to say a word," Irene giggles, her amusement infectious. As she recounts a tale from the past, she paints a vivid picture of her son Benjamin's mischievousness. As a baby, he dropped her computer, phone, and even her precious MacBook into the bathtub.

"I mean, I couldn't resist that cute little face of his when he said he just wanted to help me clean it," she adds, her laughter echoing heartily. I can't help but sympathize and share in the laughter. "Oh man, having kids is a lot," I remark, a soft laugh escaping me.

"Yeah, it is," Irene agrees with a nonchalant shrug. "But they are worth every moment of it," she says, a genuine smile gracing her face. As we stroll back to the office building after our lunch break, I bid Irene farewell as she heads to her desk. With a friendly nod, I step into the elevator, ready to head back to my office floor.

The elevator emits a gentle ding as it halts, and I step out gracefully, my stride purposeful as I make my way to my desk. Just as I'm about to settle into my seat, my attention is captivated by Alexander's office. In a heated exchange, he engages in a genuine conversation with Richard. Animated and visibly pissed. Alexander emphatically waves a document, the sound of it crashing onto the desk echoing in the air; oh shit.

I turn around and tap Chloe, whose seat is beside mine; she looks up at me, her glasses almost too big for her face, which always looks like it will fall any moment from now. Leaning in, I whisper, pointing towards the office," Any idea about what's going on in there?" pointing towards the office.

Chloe's response is a subtle, casual shrug, her muted expression revealing little. "Okay," I nod appreciatively, understanding her quiet demeanor all too well. She goes back to whatever she was doing on her laptop. At the same time, I ease myself into my seat, my attention divided between my tasks and the ongoing spectacle in Alexander' s office.

After a tense couple of minutes, my gaze locks on Richard as he emerges from Alex's office. His usually confident posture is replaced with slumped shoulders, and he seems to be massaging his temples with frustration across his features. Concern for a colleague I barely know compels me to approach him swiftly. "Hey, you okay?" I inquire, my voice laced with genuine worry.

His lips twitch into a forced smile as he glances at me, his eyes reflecting his weariness. "Yeah, just a work mishap," he explains, his voice somewhat strained as he clears his throat. I furrow my brows, taken aback by the hint of vulnerability in his response. I've never seen Alex lash out in this manner. "Got to get back to work," Richard murmurs, his warm brown eyes slightly glassy. "Thank you for asking," he adds, a touch of sincerity in his voice.

"Anytime," I whisper, reassuring as he moves away, the weight of his emotions hanging in the air.

Finally, the day draws to a close, a relentless march of time that has drained me. The clock hands indicate past 6 pm; it's getting late. Rain dances upon the windows, a gentle drizzle that's been persistent throughout the day. I cast a longing look outside, hoping the rain won't escalate into a downpour. My thoughts are selfish—wrapped up in a desire to reach home, sink into my bed, and escape into sleep's embrace. Is that too much to ask for?

The elevator's metallic doors slide shut, carrying me downward. Simon, the security guard stationed by the exit, greets me with a concerned expression. "You've been working late a lot recently, ma'am," he notes, his voice tinged with empathy and curiosity.

A small smile tugged at the corners of my lips, "Well, you know how it is," I replied with amusement.

As I step out of the building, a biting gust of wind whips through the air, causing me to shiver involuntarily. I wrap my arms around myself, my breath visible in the chilly evening air. Simon's gaze shifts to the sky, where the rain persists unabated. "Doesn't look like the rain's going to let up anytime soon," he observes, his voice carrying a tinge of sympathy.

He offers, "Shall I call a taxi for you, ma'am?" The temptation is there, but I wave off the suggestion. "No, it's okay, I'll tough it out. Thanks, Simon," I decline, mindful of how the taxi fares seem to be draining my pockets. I'll take the bus tonight.

"Perhaps you have an umbrella?" I ask. Simon shakes his head apologetically, and a sigh escapes me. This day keeps getting better and better.

Just as a mild sense of dread settles in, a sudden screech of tires pierces the air. A car skids to a halt, and the door swings open, revealing an umbrella peeking out. "Miss Olivia?" a familiar voice calls out, immediately dispelling my concerns. It's Dante, his presence accompanied by a surge of joy that lights up my face. "Dante? Oh, it's so good to see you!" I exclaim, a genuine smile breaking free.

Our embrace is warm and heartfelt. As we step back, his eyes twinkle, and his lips curl into a charming smile that makes my heart flutter.

It's good to see you too! I had no idea you were back and working here now," he says, his Italian accent seeping through.

"Oh, goodness gracious, you kids were so little when that incident happened," Dante's voice quivers, his eyes glistening with emotions he struggles to contain. "If only I were able to help..."

I place a gentle hand on his arm, offering a reassuring touch. "Oh, don't you dare get emotional on me right now," I playfully say, attempting to lighten the heavy air between us. "You couldn't have done anything. It's okay," I assure him with a warm smile.

A tender smile breaks across his face as he listens to my words, and a soft chuckle escapes him. "Besides, Camila told me how much you missed us," I continue, my voice gentle and understanding, "and how you'd always buy two chocolates, one for her and me, thinking I was still around. I know how much you cared for me, Dante, and I appreciate that."

His eyes shimmer as he nods, a mixture of gratitude and a hint of sadness in his gaze. "What can I say? I am getting old," he jokes, his voice cracking slightly as he tries to mask his emotions with humor.

Our laughter bubbles up, but a commanding voice behind us abruptly silences its mirthful melody. "Let's go, Dante," the voice calls, and I turn to see Alexander approaching, his presence eclipsing the moment.

Despite the rain's chill, an unexpected warmth unfurls within me, emanating solely from Alex's nearness. His eyes fix upon me, holding a weight of unspoken thoughts and emotions, but his lips remain sealed. A curious mixture of longing and regret swirls in his gaze, and I recognize the unresolved tension between us.

I swallow the lump threatening to rise in my throat, determined not to let him see the turmoil he stirs within me. With practiced ease, I summon a smile, masking the ache that lingers beneath the surface. I refuse to grant him the satisfaction of witnessing how deeply he affects me
.

If he chooses to behave callously, to be an ass hidden behind a veneer of detachment, then so be it. My heart clenches at the injustice of it all, at the fact that he holds such power over me. But I stand my ground, my resolve unshaken. He doesn't deserve to see the effect he has on me.

With deliberate steps, Alex makes his way toward his waiting car, Dante following in quick pursuit, the protective umbrella shielding him from the rain's persistent dance. A tiny ember of hope flickers within me, a silent yearning that he would offer me a ride home. Is anything possible? But that flicker dwindles as reality sets in.

Alex's form remains resolute. He doesn't cast a glance back. A pang of disappointment settles in my chest as I realize he won't offer a ride or even bid me goodnight.

My heart aches with the void of his absence, the silence echoing his unspoken words. Without a backward glance, he slips into the confines of his car, his expression unreadable as he closes the door. Dante, ever the gentle presence, conveys a wordless gesture of farewell, mouthing "goodnight" in a gesture that echoes with warmth.

As the car pulls away, the sound of tires against wet pavement fades into the distance, leaving me alone on the rain-soaked sidewalk.

Chapter 10

Alexander

Tuesdays! Fuck Tuesdays. Fuck any day that I must see Olivia. I'm a businessman twice her age; her brother is my best friend, and she is my daughter's best friend. I'm supposed to be like, I don't know, a father figure to her. But recently, the thoughts I've been having about her are so depraved and inappropriate.

I want to see her writhing beneath me in pleasure; her skin flushed and sweaty, and taste her in every way possible. I can only imagine how delicious she must taste. I want to sink my rigid cock into her tight hot vagina and feel her gripping me like a vice. I want to do a lot of dirty and sinful things to Olivia.

I'm supposed to be her boss, someone Abel had put in charge of her care. Not the person who'd had woken up this morning, grinding his hips into the mattress, because he had intense desires for her.

Guilt worms through me at the memory. I'm going to hell; there's no way I won't. Because as guilty as I feel, I don't think I'd be able to control myself if I continued to see her every day in my office, wearing those skirts that show her thick thighs that I want to take a nap on, oh, those curves, with that rounded butt.

No, that's not quite right. I CAN control myself around her - I just don't want to. I don't want to give up the right to carry her voice and story in my mind. I want to see my marks imprinted all over her skin, mark her whole body with loving hickeys. I want to wake up every morning with her warm body wrapped against mine and feel her pussy come all over my face. I want to drown in her beautiful scent and feel her beside me. Shit! I clench my eyes shut tightly and grit my teeth even harder.

My member swells almost impossibly harder, straining against my pants. Right now, it'd take a little action to pull down the zip, take it out, and pleasure myself while watching her from across the office. She wouldn't even know. She would not see me erupting and buckling to my lewd imagination about her. But I don't. I can't. I'm no good for her

.

Olivia truly deserves a partner who treats her as royalty, handling her delicately as a porcelain doll and adoring her every step. She deserves this person who doesn't carry my tainted history, which could only cast a shadow on her purity.

"Hi, Dad!" Camila greets me cheerfully, a wide grin lighting up her face as she enters my office. "Hey, sweetheart," I respond warmly, my voice carrying a hint of amusement. "You've been visiting my office quite frequently lately. Is everything all right?" I ask, a playful smile tugging at the corners of my lips.

"Wow, I'm offended, Dad," Camila gasps playfully, taking a few steps further into the room before settling onto the couch. "I can't come just to admire your handsome face anymore?" she teases, her eyes sparkling mischievously.

"Of course, sweetheart," I assure her with a chuckle, shaking my head in mock seriousness. "You're welcome here anytime. Although I have noticed you tend to drop by mostly when you need something," I remark, raising an eyebrow teasingly.

She shrugs and gives me an innocent pout, her lips forming an endearing expression. "Well, Daddy dearest, I do want something. I'm here to take you to lunch."

"Lunch?" I inquire, studying her with a thoughtful gaze. Her brown hair is neatly tied back in a ponytail, and her attire—a crisp white shirt paired with a brown jacket and sleek black pants—exudes professionalism that mirrors her success as an accountant.

Seeing Camila thrive in her chosen field is a source of pride and admiration. It was difficult for me to accept when she expressed her desire not to work in my company. Building this business from the ground up had been a significant part of my life, and her decision felt like a bittersweet divergence from my hopes.

Despite my initial disappointment, I had come to respect her determination. Convincing her to join the company would have been a gratifying prospect, but supporting her pursuit of happiness was more important. So, even though I wished she'd chosen to work alongside me, I understood her path and had to let her follow it.

"Yes, lunch," she states, her voice carrying a delicate inflection, "And it's with Olivia," she adds. As her name is uttered, a shiver courses through me—a reaction impossible to suppress. "I've got a few tasks to tend to, so you two can go ahead," I offer, striving to make my reluctance sound plausible. "Come on, Dad, don't be such a spoilsport. It's been a while since we hung out; don't you miss me?" Her question bears a hint of sadness, tugging at my heart. "You know I miss you, sweetheart, but it's just—" "Save me the 'I'm occupied' excuse," she interrupts, her voice playfully mimicking mine. Firmness laces her tone as she continues, "I genuinely want to spend time with you, Dad." "Okay", I say softly.

The door swings gracefully, ushered by the doorman, as the tantalizing aroma of garlic bread wafts through the air. "It's a pleasure to see you, Mr. McQueen!" Alejandro's jovial voice resonates from the right, accompanied by hearty chuckles. With purposeful strides, he approaches, extending his hand for a handshake while a genuine smile illuminates his features. Crinkles grace the corners of his eyes, his once-dark hair now a graceful hue of grey and hinting at an impending receding hairline.

"It's truly my pleasure to be here, Alejandro, and I've always insisted you call me Alex," I reply warmly. He waves off my words, his grey eyes momentarily wandering behind me before settling back on our gathering. "And who might these lovely companions be?" he inquires with an intrigued twinkle.

A dulcet tone carries over as Camila steps forward, enveloping Alejandro in a heartfelt embrace. "Lovely to see you too, Alejandro," she offers gracefully. His compliment flows effortlessly, his grin unwavering. "With each meeting, your beauty only grows," he playfully remarks, a gentle blush gracing Camila's cheeks. Alejandro's charm remains undiminished over time, and sometimes, I wonder how his wife deals with his charming ways.

His Curious eyes land on Olivia, prompting his inquiry about her identity. With poise, Olivia introduced herself as my assistant, extending her hand for a handshake. His reaction, however, surpasses convention as he warmly embraces her. "Ah, dear heavens, you're a vision!" he exclaims, leaving Olivia visibly touched by his charm.

"Thank you, Mr. Alejandro," Olivia says, her voice carrying a soft giggle and a faint blush gracing her cheeks. With a charming smile, Alejandro responds, "Oh, please, call me Alejandro." Catching his friendly tone, Olivia nods and replies, "Okay, Alejandro."

With an inviting gesture, Alejandro adds, "Come on! Let me show you to your table."

"Hey, remember when Oscar mustered the courage to ask you out? I couldn't believe it when you told me he placed a dozen roses on your front porch and even spent the night until your brother intervened and sent him away. Oh my God, I still burst into laughter thinking about it!" Camila says, prompting an infectious giggle from Olivia.

Meanwhile, I am jabbing the knife into my steak with increasing force, observing the succulent juices cascading onto the pristine white plate beneath. Each chew feels almost aggressive like I'm channeling all my frustration.

I am stewing.

My mother used to make this god-awful stew when I was young. It smelt like a dumpster fire and tasted even worse. My attitude is about as foul as that stew right now.

My fingers reach out, curling around the delicate stem of the wine glass. I lift it to my lips with determined swiftness, consuming its contents in a desperate gulp. The cold liquid rushes down my throat, a momentary respite from the weight of the situation.

A persistent longing for something more substantial tugs at my mind, an insistent itch I struggle to ignore. But I make a silent promise to satisfy that yearning at a more fitting time.

Seated amidst the hum of conversation and the clatter of utensils, I observe in silence as Camila runs through every man who has asked Olivia out and the ones she gave a chance to, and the more I hear, the more my grip tightens on the knife and fork I'm holding.

I have always prided myself on my aversion to violence, preferring the path of diplomacy and self-restraint. Yet, in this charged moment, a dark thought of giving in to aggression creeps into my mind like an ominous shadow.

"You've been silent for a while, Dad, what's wrong?" Camila's voice breaks the settled silence, jolting me from my reverie. My eyes lift abruptly, meeting her concerned gaze. With a discreet throat clearing, I muster a response, "Oh, it's nothing. I just thought I'd let you girls catch up." My words roll forth, as smooth as gravel but veiling the unease within.

Olivia's voice interjects, her attention on the garlic bread before her, "You don't have to stay if you don't want to." Her statement hangs in the air. Perplexed, I inquire, my tone firming slightly, "What do you mean?" Her eyes meet mine, and a subtle shrug accompanies her words, "I mean, you must have a mountain of tasks at the office. It's all right to go and tend to them."

"I don't think," I begin to say, my words suspended in the air, only to be abruptly halted as the waiter gracefully glides over to our table, his presence demanding attention as he reaches to collect the bill. At that moment, his gaze lingers too long on Olivia. As he expertly refills her wine glass, a small slip of paper stealthily descends, finding its place upon her thighs. It's an action that is so subtle that anyone could have missed it. But I didn't because my attention was on her.

"The wine is on the house," he says, sneaking another glance at Olivia. With a strained smile, I mutter, "Sure, pass along my thanks to Alejandro." I watch him retreat, my gaze fixed on his departing figure. I'm teetering on edge, tempted to upend this entire lunch and whisk Olivia away, but I can't risk arousing Camila's suspicions, no matter how badly I want to.

Camila's voice chimes, "Oh my God, that's adorable!" She's enamored by the note Olivia holds. I muster a casual tone, asking, "What's that?"

Olivia dismisses it, "Oh, it's nothing." Folding the paper, she conceals its contents.

Camila's excitement is palpable as she exclaims, "What do you mean 'nothing'? Tell him!" Turning towards me, she says, "Dad, he gave her his number and said he'd like to hang out with her; it's so sweet!"

I nod at Olivia, masking my discomfort as I say, "You should give him a shot; he seems like a good kid." The words feel acrid and forced, a bitter pill to swallow. But if Olivia found someone else, it might cause me to keep my distance. My thoughts twist, and I clench my teeth; it never stopped me before.

Regardless of their relationship status, I pursued women and slept with them without hesitation.

"Yeah, I'll give him a chance," Olivia says, her green eyes looking intently at me.

Chapter 11

Olivia

The morning sun streams through the curtains, casting a golden hue across the room as I stumble out of bed. A hot shower after waking up didn't help scald away any of my frustration. Nor did the brushing through the tangles of my hair harder than intended.

Walking to the kitchen, my feet make a soft, rhythmic padding against the floor. I measure instant coffee into a well-worn mug, adding a lot of creamer and sugar. I'd never understand those who prefer their coffee black. But Alexander likes his coffee black, my inner subconscious says, nope, shut up, I silently admonish my inner subconscious. You know you'll continue to think about him all day, right? It's all you do, the snarky little voice continues. Whose side is this bitch on?

"No, no," I mutter, lightly slapping my face to dispel the intrusive thoughts. A harsh exhale escapes my lips. "Today, there won't be a single thought of Alex, none at all, yes," I affirm with a determined nod, my voice echoing through the silence of the apartment.

A deep sigh escapes my lips as I go over to the couch, coffee in hand, and careful not to tip over the new flower vase I got. Please don't ask me why. I love the sight of flowers around the house.

Something about those delicate blooms scattered around the apartment makes this place, which I can barely consider a home, feel somewhat improved. In the future, when I've saved enough money, I plan to escape this hell hole for good.

With the hot cup of coffee cradled in my hands, I bring it to my lips and take a soothing sip. My laptop awaits on the table, its black screen reflecting the dim room around me. I click the virtual link to connect with Abel for our scheduled video call.

The circle on the screen stirs to life, rolling for a fleeting moment before his face comes on.

"Hey, what's up?" His voice calls out, sounding slightly distorted over the screen, but I can still hear him quite well.

"Missed me?" I ask teasingly, my lips turning up into a smile.

"Pfft... you wish," he snorts, his nose scrunching up in his usual manner. It was a habit that had always made him seem like a snob, although I'd never tell him that.

"You know, it's been a while since you've been graced with looking at this pretty face. It would be best if you were honored," I say, a playful giggle escaping my lips as I take another sip of the coffee.

"Oh, please," he laughs, his eyes crinkling at the corners. "Trust me, I see you every time I look in the mirror. You're like my reflection. Keep your honor to yourself, please."

It was true. We looked so alike that sometimes people mistook me for his daughter, offering their sympathy to him, assuming he was a single father. Our hair shared the same hue, auburn, and our eyes, a vibrant shade of green, were an inheritance from our mother.

Our only distinguishing feature was our skin – mine, an olive complexion, and Abel's, tanned from a lifetime spent under the sun. Witnessing Abel's reaction when such mistaken assumptions occurred always amused me. He'd become visibly flustered, struggling to explain our actual relationship. Eventually, we grew tired of correcting others and letting them believe what they wished.

"So, uh, I heard you're working for Alex now?" He asks his gaze intent on me. I knew this was coming; I didn't know it'd be so soon. A sharp exhale escapes my mouth, and I say, "Yeah, it just happened that way."

"But, why didn't you tell me?" He asks, a frown etched on his face. "I thought we shared everything, Cara Mia?" There's a touch of hurt in his voice. "Cara Mia," he started calling me after we watched a cartoon where her brother addressed the main character like that. He said she looked like me, and he liked the name too, though I couldn't see the resemblance. I thought he was teasing me, and I hated that name for years, but now? I love it.

"Yeah, uhm... I was going to tell you. I just wanted to, you know, settle in," I stammer, trying to sound convincing. He raises an eyebrow, clearly skeptical. I am full of shit, and we both know it.

I knew he'd resist, saying, ' I don't want you to bother them; you can do this alone". Guess what? I already tried that route. It led me to scrape by in a café, dealing with entitled elderly patrons. Sorry, Patty.

"Listen, I know I may not be the most logical voice of reasoning sometimes," he begins.

"You mean all the time," I interject.

"Sometimes," he states firmly, his tone hardening.

"Just kidding," I mutter, sheepish.

"But, before you do something like this, I'd appreciate it if you'd let me know in advance. I had to hear it from a friend there."

"You have friends other than Alex?" I ask, giggling. My brother rarely calls anyone a friend, except for Alex. He doesn't exactly exude friendliness with his permanent scowl. Seriously, we need to work on that.

"Olivia!" He snaps, frustration evident in his voice. If he were here, he'd probably knock some sense into me.

Geez, okay! All right! Don't put your panties in a twist."

He sighs deeply, his chest heaving. Shaking his head, he mutters, "What will I do with you?"

I stick out my tongue with a silly grin. "You love me. And, it's okay, I love you too, bro."

"In your dreams," he rolls his eyes. "Is he treating you well?" he asks.

"Yeah, of course he is," I reply, nodding and averting my gaze from the screen. I can't let my brother see how Alex's mere thought creates butterflies in my stomach, how his handsome face invades my thoughts, how every little thing he does affects me. I can't let him know I'm falling for Alex.

That, I'm beginning to fall for the way he curls up his lips in distaste when there's something wrong with any document, or when he furrows his eyebrows when he's in thought and sucks his lower lip, unconsciously, or how I discreetly sniff the musky scent he always has on him, any time we're together. Alex is an enigma, and I'm more than willing to get to know and understand him.

"Olivia," my brother calls my name in a warning tone. Bringing my eyes back to the screen, with as much enthusiasm and confidence as I could muster, I say, "I'm enjoying it there, Abel, and he's treating me well. Look at it: his company is one of the best, and working there is a dream for me, and you know that. So, please be happy for me about this, hmm?"

"Fine," he grunts, "but if anything happens, you're leaving, okay?" What could happen?

"Why are you so against me working at Alexander's company?" I ask, my voice laced with suspicion.

Alex was my brother's best friend, and he trusted no one else to care for me. So, why was he acting this way?

"It's nothing," he averts his gaze, "I'm just looking out for you, Olivia, that's it," hmmm. "Sure."

"Listen, I –"I begin to say when I'm cut short by a ball hitting my window, making a loud crashing noise and breaking. It's the ball rolling in; what the hell?

"What the hell was that," Abel shouts, his voice frantic. "I'll check it out; I'll talk to you later,"

"But, Olivia!" I slap the laptop shut and walk to the window, careful not to step on any shard of glass on the floor.

My gaze falls on the basketball ball; sitting in the corner of my kitchen, narrowing my eye on it, I see a little bit of a black mark on it; I recognize that ball. "It better not be what I'm thinking," I mutter.

Looking through my window, the streets below look empty, with no sign of anyone playing basketball or anything. "Oh, so now you hide. After crashing through my window, you hide like a coward. You had better come out here, and let's talk about this civilly before I call the cops!" I probably look like a madwoman yelling through the window, but I don't care. I am not fixing this window with my money.

My eyes catch a movement beneath the red car across the street. Narrowing my gaze, I see a pair of sneakers under the car, moving. "What the hell?"

The red sneakers move slowly, emerging from the car's protective shadow, revealing Michael. "You've got to be kidding me," I mutter. A sheepish grin stretches across his face as he raises his hand in a casual wave.

"Hi, Olivia!" he shouts, his voice carrying an odd mix of excitement and guilt.

"Are you kidding me right now?" I yell back, a surge of anger coursing through my veins. Stalking me isn't enough; he just has to break my window.

"Bye, Olivia!" Michael calls out, and before I can react, he bolts down the street, running hard and fast without a single backward glance.

My mouth forms an O, hanging open like a catfish in disbelief. Despite the absurdity of the situation, a deep chortle escapes my lips.

Chapter 12

Alexander

It's early. Too early.

Nursing my glass of whiskey, I sit in the dimly lit corner of an upscale bar. The sun has barely risen, and the world is beginning to stir. I swirl the amber liquid in my glass, my eyes unfocused as I try to make sense of the storm raging inside me.

In my forty-three years, I have faced countless challenges in the business world, but none has left me as disoriented as this one. I could no longer deny the truth; I was interested in someone I shouldn't be.

My fingers clenched around the crystal tumbler, the ice cubes clinking softly against the glass.

It is a dangerous affair, harboring feelings for someone I shouldn't, especially when that someone was my best friend's younger sister and my daughter's best friend.

I can't shake her image from my mind – those captivating green eyes that hold innocence and wisdom, her radiant smile that could light up the darkest boardroom.

She has been my assistant for the past three months, and her competence and grace make her indispensable to my daily life. But it isn't just her professionalism that has captivated me. It's her smile, her laughter filling the room, and the warmth in her eyes when she looks at me.

The weight of the situation presses down on my shoulders. I know I can't let my feelings for Olivia grow any more substantial, yet I can't seem to stop them. The line between friendship, professionalism, and desire has blurred, and I'm teetering on the edge of a precipice I can't afford to fall from.

I down my drink, the burn of the alcohol temporarily drowning out the turmoil within. I have worked too hard to build my empire and will not jeopardize it all for a forbidden attraction.

"Shouldn't you be at your office?" Ben says flatly. His sparkling black dress shoes come into my view as I slowly raise my glossy eyes to look at his face, which wears a blank stare. Only Thomas's poker face can put my poker face to shame.

"Shouldn't you be working?" I ask wryly.

"I am working. But, there's a grown man here, in my club, drunk at 6 a.m. It's not exactly a sight for sore eyes," he snaps.

"Well, you do have sore eyes," I say, my voice groggy. He narrows his gaze on me, the most reaction I'd get.

Grunting, I stand to my feet, swaying a bit. "You're a spoilsport," I mutter sloppily.

The dimly lit room seemed to come to life as the early morning sun struggled to infiltrate the thick curtains.

Groaning heavily, I extract my phone from the inner pocket of my waistcoat, fumbling with the device before finally dialing Dante's number. The recollection of instructing him to leave last night, right after he'd dropped me off at this place, flashes through my hazy mind. But now, I desperately need him to take me to work.

Dante's voice cuts through the fog of my hangover, reassuring and swift as he promises to arrive in five minutes.

Swaying gently on my unsteady feet, I collide with a few barstools, the relentless throbbing in my head a cruel reminder of my action overnight. With grim determination, I navigate through the dimly lit room. Ben's curses follow me like a haunting chorus as I escape.

The morning air is tense as my car stops before the club. Dante steps out first, his silent disapproval hanging in the air. He opens the car door for me, his lips forming a tight line and his face etched with a stern frown. Without a word, I enter the car, and Dante takes the driver's seat, steering us towards the office.

As we arrive at the building, Irene casts a concerned gaze. Her worry is evident, but she doesn't abandon her post or approach me. My unsteady legs carry me to the elevator, and I press the button for the top floor. Leaning against the cold metal, I can feel the alcohol-induced haze in my head gradually dissipating.

My throat is dry and scratchy, a reminder of the night's indulgence, but I always sober up quickly despite the drinks. It's a peculiar talent, a blessing in disguise, but it felt more like a curse right now.

As I leave, the elevator emits a soft ding, my footsteps echoing through the quiet office corridor. It's still early, and only a handful of my employees have arrived, their desks largely vacant.

I settle into the plush chair behind my desk, a sense of weariness washing over me. With a deft motion, I open the bottom drawer, revealing a small container of hangover pills Irene had thoughtfully purchased some time ago.

Retrieving one, I make my way to the compact mini-fridge nearby. Carefully, I extract a chilled bottle of water, the condensation slipping between my fingers as I uncap it.

The pill is placed in my mouth, and I wash it with a grimace, my aversion to medicine evident. Oddly, for an adult, I've never quite conquered my hate of medication; I'd even take an injection over pills any day.

A heavy sigh escapes my lips as I sink into the comfort of the nearby couch. I reach for the remote to lower the blinds, casting the room into dim, soothing darkness, and then, I shield my eyes with my forearm, sensing a migraine on the horizon.

The thought weighs heavily: I need to reduce my drinking. Time's ticking, and I'm not getting any younger.

"Good morning, Mr. McQueen!" Olivia's cheerful voice slices through the sleep I was gradually succumbing to. "What?" I mumble groggily, rubbing my eyes with the palms of my hands and reluctantly sitting up on the couch. "What the hell are you doing here so early?" I inquire without bothering to lift my gaze to meet hers.

"It's 9 am, Sir," she replies.

What? How is it that precisely when I decided to steal a few moments of sleep, time chose to sprint ahead? Sometimes, I can't help but wonder if I wronged a king in a past life, and his vengeful family is pursuing me.

"Um, should I make a cup of coffee for you?" Olivia ventures, her tone cautious. Undoubtedly, she's contemplating the peculiarity of her boss being in the office, clearly nursing a hangover so early in the morning. A small smile tugs at my lips. If only she knew.

Nodding slightly, I start to say, "Yes, please, you can..." but my words trail off as I finally raise my head to look at her. She's clad in a sundress, its slender straps delicately hugging her shoulders. At the same time, it flows gracefully just above her knees, accentuating her delicate figure—the sweetheart neckline teases, offering a glimpse of her whole breast enticingly against the fabric.

I swallow hard as my gaze drifts down to her legs, encased in a pair of brown sandals that adorn her feet like a work of art. I never considered myself to have a foot fetish, but at this moment, I think I might have developed one.

"Is there an event I'm not aware of?" I ask.

"Oh, this?" She responds, her gaze drifting down to her dress. The simple action causes a stray strand of her hair to escape from the messy bun she's fashioned it into. My fingers itch on my thighs, and I have a subtle urge to reach out and tuck it back into place.

"Today is the staff's picnic day. And I was told we could wear anything we wanted, as long as it was appropriate," she explains, her eyes finding mine.

I had forgotten entirely about that annual event, an idea I had conjured up ostensibly to show appreciation to the staff, giving them a day of respite. But truthfully, it was just a way to keep them out of my hair.

Over the years, I never accompanied them to these outings or any other activities they organized, even though a few had extended invitations. I suspect those were merely polite gestures. No one, I'm confident, wants to spend their day off in the company of their perpetually sour-faced boss.

Yet, an unexpected temptation creeps in as I gaze at Olivia in that dress. I imagine the multitude of wandering eyes that will undoubtedly be drawn to her, and she'll remain blissfully oblivious to her beauty.

She'd try to be pleasant, engage in conversations, smile – all those pleasantries – without inkling the sinful thoughts concealed behind those polite exchanges. I'm a man; I know how these things work.

"It's that bad?" she asks, her voice carrying a hint of disappointment, and then she rushes to add, "I can change if you want me to," her gaze nervously diverting from me. "I don't know what I was thinking; I shouldn't have worn this to work," she mumbles softly beneath her breath.

"No, it's not," I respond, my eyes locked onto her, appreciating how a delicate blush tints her cheeks. "You look wonderful in it."

A heartfelt "Thank you" escapes her lips, spoken quietly, as if she's grappling with the unexpected compliment.

But then, a thought occurs to me, so ludicrous that it almost feels absurdly daring. "Did you wear this for me today, Olivia?" I inquire, my voice taking on a husky undertone.

Her lips parted slightly, her eyes widening just a fraction, and the blush deepened on her cheeks. "I don't understand," she whispers.

I rise to my full height, moving deliberately toward her, and I observe as she takes a step back, her eyes wide with uncertainty. "You could have simply gone to the picnic, you know. There was no need for you to come in here at all. So, why did you, hmm?" I question.

"I just wanted to do my job as your assistant," she responds, her voice quivering slightly. "Your window blinds were closed, and I wondered if you were already in. When I entered, it was clear you were hungover, and I thought you might need a cup of coffee, so I asked," Her voice drops to a whisper as I close the distance between us, pressing her gently against the door with a soft thud.

She gazes back at me, realizing there's nowhere to escape to. Her eyes meet mine, now burning with an intense heat.

"My window blinds were closed. You could have assumed I wasn't in the office. And as for the coffee, I'm quite capable of making it myself, as I've done countless times before," I murmur, my shoulders lifting in a nonchalant shrug.

My fingers graze the crimson-coated contours of her lower lip, and an instinctual urge to smudge that lipstick consumes me. "You know why you came in here, Olivia?" I whisper, my breath tantalizingly close to her face. Leaning closer, I use my thigh to nudge her legs apart, settling it between hers, eliciting a soft gasp as she leans into me. "Because you wanted me to see you like this. You dressed up for me. And do you have any idea how that makes me feel? To witness how utterly irresistible you look right now?"

I run my tongue along the curve of her ear, gently nipping her earlobe between my teeth. My words spill out in a husky murmur, "It drives me wild." She responds with a moan and a whimper, her breasts pressed invitingly against my chest, igniting a surge of desire.

Nuzzling into her neck, I leave open-mouthed kisses along her skin, savoring the sweet scent of vanilla that emanates from her. "But you know what pisses me off?" I inquire, tugging harshly at her skin with my teeth.

"Oh God," she moans, her voice quivering.

"It's the fact that other men will be ogling you, unable to tear their eyes away, wishing you were theirs," I growl, gripping her luscious ass firmly, kneading it with purpose.

Leaning back, I fix my gaze on her, my finger lingering inside her mouth, traces of her saliva clinging to it, her once pristine red lipstick now a smudged testament to our vibrant encounter. Her eyes, however, reveal a potent mix of longing and desire as I speak with unwavering resolve.

"But, I'm not bothered. Do you know why? Because you belong to me. Do you understand that?" I assert firmly.

Without further hesitation, I capture her lips with an unbridled passion. Grinding her against my growing arousal, I swallow each of her delicate moans and whispered whimpers. This moment surpasses even my wildest expectations and imaginations. Coaxing her mouth to open, I delve deep with my tongue, igniting a fire between us.

But then, abruptly, she draws back, pushing me away with an urgency born of intense desire. She breathes heavily, her words emerging in strained gasps, "I shouldn't have allowed this to happen. You're still drunk and probably won't think much of this."

Her eyes betray her undeniable hunger, mirroring the longing burning within me.

"I... I have to go now," she stammers, hastily retreating from the office.

Chapter 13

Olivia

"Oh my God, you will love this so much!" Irene gushes beside me, her face excitedly as we pack the frozen sandwiches I prepared at home while she carefully arranges the wines into a picnic basket.

"It's just a picnic, Irene. I don't think there will be much to enjoy," I reply with a slight smile.

"Just a picnic." Irene gasps dramatically, placing her hands over her chest, her eyes widening. "We are attending the most prestigious picnic of the century, set in the most luxurious location in all of Chicago, and you're calling it 'just a picnic'?"

"It's taking place in an open-air public garden. I doubt it will be as grand or prestigious as you make it sound," I deadpan in response.

"Urgh... you're such a downer," she mumbles, her nose wrinkling slightly. "What's wrong with you, anyway? You've been acting all strange since this morning."

"Nothing," I reply swiftly, my eyes focused on the sandwiches as I try to avoid Irene's penetrating gaze.

"You sure?" she inquires, casting me a sidelong glance.

"Yeah, I'm good," I assure her, stealing a glance and offering a small smile.

"Okay," she concedes, though her skepticism is evident. She doesn't press further, and I'm thankful for that.

The last thing I want is to dwell on what transpired in Alex's office. My lips still tingle with the memory, and I'd instead not think about it.

"I suppose you guys are ready?" Richard asks, his eyes shifting from Irene to me, taking in the baskets we hold. Since neither Irene nor I can access a car, he generously offered to drive us to our picnic spot this sunny day.

"Come on! The picnic awaits us!" Irene's voice bubbles with excitement as she practically skips toward Richard's car. My eyes meet Richard's, and we share a brief, knowing laugh.

The atmosphere is alive with the symphony of birdsong, punctuated by the laughter and giggles of other picnickers. Various foods and snacks spill from open containers, and the sun's relentless rays bathe us in warmth. At least it isn't raining, with a hint of relief.

"Come on, guys, our spot is over there," Richard announces, gesturing toward a secluded area in the park. With a helping hand, he assists us in unloading our picnic gear. Together, we pass through the lush greenery, passing families and couples lounging on the soft grass, seeking their slice of outdoor bliss.

"Hey guys, you're here," Isabella waves us over as we take our seats on the blankets on the lush green grass.

"This looks nice," I say, setting out the sandwiches and arranging them neatly in the large box at the center of our little circle, where the spread of food awaits.

"Definitely. I always look forward to this. It's such a nice way to unwind," Isabella remarks, a subtle smile on her lips.

"Also, it's very generous of Mr. McQueen. Not all CEOs would have the initiative to give their workers a day off, let alone agree to this yearly picnic," she adds.

"Yeah, he is," I mutter, forcing a small smile onto my face.

I lock eyes with Irene as she hands me an opened bottle of fruit wine, her eyebrows furrowed in concern. I respond with another strained smile and give her a slight shake of my head, silently conveying that I'm okay.

"This is boring," Isabella declares suddenly, her nose wrinkling in distaste. "Let's go do something fun," she urges, her voice imbued with mischief and excitement.

A harmonious chorus of "Yeah, we should!" echoes from the other employees.

Rising from her seat and elegantly brushing the hem of her shorts, Isabella's jet-black hair dances in the wind, framing her face as she shields her eyes from the sun's rays with her hands. "We could try the 'Wheel of Death,'" she proposes with a sly grin, her gaze encompassing all of us.

"' Wheel of death?'" I question, my curiosity piqued.

"Yeah, it's right over there," She points to the other side of the garden, where a small white gate stands, revealing a colossal drop tower, ominously stationary.

"Uhh... no thanks," I reply hesitantly, my throat constricting. There's no way I'm getting on that thing.

"You sure?" Irene inquires.

"Yeah, I'm going to sit this one out," I affirm.

"And I'm terrified of heights, so, no," Richard chimes in horrifyingly. It's so comical that I can't help but release a small giggle.

"Suit yourselves! Come on, everyone, let's go!" Isabella exclaims with infectious excitement, and they all eagerly follow her lead.

"Here, have this," Richard presents a red velvet cupcake, a tempting aroma dancing before my face.

"Thank you," I reply, accepting it from his hands. As I take a bite, a surprised hum escapes my lips. My eyes widen, and I can't help but ask, "Did you make this? It's amazing."

A shy smile graces Richard's lips as he confirms, "Yeah, I did."

"Oh my God," I mumble between mouthfuls, "I had no idea you baked," my voice lighthearted.

"It's one of my hidden talents," he admits.

"I think my talent would be eating this for the rest of my life," I confess, giggling. "I love cakes, and this has to be the best one I've ever had, no kidding."

"Okay, stop! You're going to make my head swell at this rate," he teases, a short laugh escaping his lips.

"So, mind telling me what's been on your mind all day?" He asks, his warm brown eyes on me.

My brow furrows in confusion. "What do you mean?" I ask, wrapping the half-eaten cupcake in a napkin.

He sees through my façade, speaking gently, "You don't fool me, Olivia. You've been drifting in and out of conversations all day, wearing that faraway look in your eyes as if something's been bothering you, something you can't stop thinking about."

Drawing deep breaths, my chest rising and falling, I contemplate seeking a third-party opinion. "What would you do," I inquire cautiously, turning fully towards him with my legs folded beneath me, "if you liked someone and believed they felt the same, but they won't admit it?"

Richard pauses, his bottom lip disappearing into his mouth as he scratches his chin thoughtfully with his fingers. "Has he told you he likes you?" he finally asks.

"No, he has not," I respond.

But I know he does. He wouldn't have kissed me like he did if there wasn't some attraction. 'But he was drunk,' my subconscious offers its dissenting opinion. Drunk or not, Alexander knew exactly what he was doing.

"You are a wonderful woman, Olivia," he sighs, his voice tinged with admiration. "Any man would be fortunate to have you as their own. But, on this matter, I believe you should ask him directly if he likes you or not. It appears that he's sending you mixed signals, causing confusion. And that's not a desirable trait in a man, in my opinion," he remarks, a faint frown creasing his features.

"Just ask him. It can't be that difficult," he suggests with a nonchalant shrug.

"But oh, Richard, it is difficult," I muse silently. Confronting Alex like that might push him further away, and that would undo the progress I have made.

I can't fathom what has prompted him to be so open about his feelings, but I am determined not to sabotage it. I will take my time and unravel the enigma that is Alexander.

"Thank you, Richard," I express, a small smile gracing my lips.

"You're welcome," he replies, his expression mirroring my gratitude.

"Guys!" Irene suddenly yells, sprinting toward us from the other side, breathless and with her hair clinging to her sweaty skin.

Rising in haste, I ask, "Hey, what's wrong? What happened?"

"Isabella broke her foot."

Chapter 14

Alexander

I was six years old when I had my first kiss. It happened with Clarissa, a girl in second grade. I remember how her mouth tasted like garlic. However, the unforgiving constraints of her braces confined our exploration to the realm of modest, closed-mouth kisses.

I didn't speak to her again after that.

I had my second kiss in junior high with a senior. She tasted like cinnamon, and I accidentally bit her on the lips, making it bleed.

Panic coursed through her, and she fled the scene, leaving me to grapple with the situation's complexity.

The remembrance of the kiss is etched in my mind like a sepia-toned photograph in a dusty album.

Over the years, my life has been painted with a mosaic of kisses, each a unique blend of good, bad, and worse, shared with women who wove their stories into mine.

Sometimes, it was just a kiss, an innocent interlude of affection. But more often than not, those kisses served as the opening chords to a symphony of passion, leading me down intriguing paths of intimacy.

Yet, here I am, a week removed from the most extraordinary kiss I've ever experienced—right in this very office. A kiss that had ignited an inferno of desire and left my senses ablaze. And yet, paradoxically, it stands as the most fleeting, vanishing before my grasp as she escaped.

The Irony cuts deep. For as long as I can recall, I had always been the one to steer these romantic encounters, the captain of my ship navigating the waters of passion. I wielded the power to halt those kisses, to deny the pursuit of more, regardless of their emotional desires.

But this time, the tables had turned. I was the one halted in my tracks, left yearning for something more, and it gnaws at me, an unfamiliar sensation that refuses to be dismissed.

Her taste lingers on my lips, a haunting memory of how her body molded seamlessly into mine, a dance of desire that left an indelible mark. The intensity of her response was so utterly intoxicating that it bordered on addictive. But I can't deny the sobering truth. That moment was a mistake, an impulsive plunge into the depths of passion driven by the haze of alcohol.

I murmur the words to myself, my voice a quiet confession, as if saying them aloud could somehow absolve the memory of its consequences.

"I need coffee," I mumble, the words barely audible in the quiet office. My outstretched hand hovers above the intercom button, poised to summon a caffeine fix, but a sudden change of heart redirects my course. No, I'll fetch it myself; a brief escape from the confines of my desk is long overdue.

Pushing up from my seat, I navigate my way toward the office door; my curiosity piqued as I glimpse Olivia rising from her chair, a stack of documents in her grasp. I find myself wondering where she's off to. With a decisive turn, she begins to stride toward my office.

"No, no, no," I mutter, my pace quickening as I retreat to my desk. I plop down just in the nick of time, an accidental collision with my desk sending a jolt of pain through my knee.

"Damn it!" I groan, clutching my throbbing leg as Olivia swings the door open.

"Is everything okay?" Olivia's concerned inquiry cuts through the awkward air, her brow slightly furrowed.

I clear my throat, trying to conceal the grimace that threatens to surface. "Yeah, everything is fine," I respond with an air of nonchalance, though I can sense the tension lingering between us.

"Okay..." She hesitates before continuing, "This is Mr. Jordan's file. It needs your signature." Her voice is steady as she extracts the file from the stack of documents clutched in her arm and places it on my desk, directly in front of me.

"Okay," I acknowledge, reaching for my pen and scribbling my signature. The transaction is swift and devoid of the usual small talk that permeates our interactions.

"Here you go," I say, returning the now-signed file to her. She accepts it, her gaze locking onto mine with an enigmatic intensity. It's a look so mysterious that I can't decipher her thoughts.

"Don't we have something to talk about?" Olivia finally breaks the silence, her words hanging in the air.

"I don't think so." I shrug, feigning ignorance, though guilt festers beneath the surface. My heart sinks at the disappointment etched across her features. I know I'm behaving like an ass, but I'd let her believe it was a drunken mistake rather than reveal the truth: she has consumed my thoughts since that kiss, and I can't stop thinking about her. I can't let her know that.

"All right," she responds, her hands trembling slightly as she places a cup of coffee on my desk, a detail I had not noticed until now. "That's your cup of coffee." Her tone is measured, and the tension lingers, unspoken words hovering between us like a forbidden secret.

"Well, if you hadn't missed our appointment yesterday,"- Daniel adjusts one of the many stacks of paper on my desk- "you wouldn't just be informed about this today."

I pinch the bridge of my nose. "I was busy," I growl.

My lawyer sighs. "Fine, fine, I'll drop it."

"Appreciate that," I say flatly.

"Well, the good news is I have rescheduled the meeting for tomorrow. It's in New York".

"What?" I push out of the now uncomfortable chair.

He may be the best lawyer in Chicago, but my patience is thinner than usual today. I considered telling him why I didn't attend the meeting yesterday and that I was busy touching myself to the memory of my kiss with Olivia, but then I decided against it.

"What do you mean by tomorrow?" I inquire, my voice tinged with a note of frustration.

His response is laden with a subtle hint of reproach. "I tried reaching out to you throughout yesterday, but since you were 'unavailable,'" he emphasizes the word with a pointed stare, "it just happened like that. So, you've got to be in New York for this deal with the Arab prince," he delivers the news with an air of calm detachment.

My jaw clenches, and my face contorts into a tight, displeased frown. I've never been fond of surprises, but this one is unavoidable.

New York beckons, and the prospect of meeting the elusive Arab prince looms.

The Intricacies of such encounters are labyrinthine, with stringent official processes to navigate, even for someone of my standing. This is my singular opportunity, for the prince is rarely outside his homeland, and now, he's gracing New York with his presence.

Daniel has done a hell of a job.

"What time is the flight?"

As we stroll toward my private plane, the low mechanical hum fills the air, and Olivia's discontent breaks the silence. "You could have told me we were going to New York tonight. I could have been more prepared," she grumbles from beside me.

I can't suppress my irritation. "Well, if I had been aware of this, I would have informed you earlier. You're not the only one inconvenienced by this," I retort sharply.

I continue, my voice laced with sarcasm, "Although I guess this wouldn't be such an inconvenience for you, considering your excitement." Without sparing her a glance, I push forward into the plane.

The weight of the impending deal with Prince Mossain has me on edge. One wrong move, and it can all come crashing down. I must maintain focus and not allow anyone's complaints or whining to distract me.

Settling down on the farthest seat in the corner of the private jet, I take out my laptop, ready to immerse myself in work. The plush leather chair cradles me as the hum of the engines fills the cabin.

"Is there anything I can do?" Olivia's voice breaks through my concentration.

I look up from my laptop and meet her gaze—a faint smile tugs at the corners of her lips. Shaking my head, I reply, "No, there's not. You can rest. It's a long flight ahead."

She nods softly, her brown eyes reflecting a hint of disappointment as she settles into the seat directly before me.

I can't help but point out, "There are other seats in the plane."

With a casual shrug, she replies, "Yeah, I know. I want to sit here in case you need anything. Is there a problem with that?" Her tone holds a touch of defiance.

Yes, there is a problem. A problem that I can't admit to. I can't focus on my work with you sitting right there in front of me. I can't get anything done with your intoxicating vanilla scent around me. I won't be able to look at your lips coated in that red shade of lipstick without thinking about how you taste.

But I don't say those things.

Raising an eyebrow instead, she meets my challenge with a defiant smile, a playful gleam in her eye. I don't understand her game, but it's undeniably intriguing.

"Okay, you can stay here," I relent, my voice calm as I return to my laptop, secretly relishing the unspoken tension between us.

A loud yawn escapes Olivia's mouth, and I can't help but chuckle softly under my breath. It was the third yawn in a row.

"You trying to swallow me whole or what?" I playfully quip, infusing my voice with teasing warmth.

"I wasn't that loud!" She protests, a faint blush coloring her cheeks and lending her an endearing vulnerability.

"Sure," I say, my tongue lightly pressed against my cheek.

"I wasn't loud!" She asserts, her defense brimming with a touch of wounded pride.

Cocking an eyebrow at her, I retort cheekily, "I didn't say a word."

"You didn't have to. It's written all over your face," she mumbles, sinking into the chair. At this moment, her face is entirely red. With her olive skin tone, I often wonder just how deep her blush must be to show so prominently on her skin.

"If anything, you look cute when you yawn," I say with a playful grin.

Clearing her throat, she whispers, "Thank you."

"What are your allergies?" I ask, my eyes fixed on my laptop screen while my fingers produce a rhythmic clacking sound on the keyboard.

"Allergies?" She queries, her face displaying a perplexed wrinkle.

"Yes, allergies," I confirm. "We'll be staying at a hotel where meals will be served, so I need to know if you have any allergies. That way, they can accommodate your dietary restrictions."

"Oh," she responds, her expression shifting to one of sudden understanding.

"Well?" I prompt.

"I'm allergic to peanut butter, and while I'm not allergic to tomatoes, I don't particularly like them," she explains.

"Tomatoes?" I ask, my surprise evident in my tone.

"Why?" I sputter. Who doesn't like tomatoes?

Another nonchalant shrug. "I don't know, they just seem so mushy and gross," she says, a visible look of disgust overtaking her features.

"And here, I thought I was the weird one for not liking ice cream," I mumble, the words escaping my lips involuntarily.

"You don't like ice cream," Olivia exclaims, her outburst drawing the curious glances of Daniel and a few other associates aboard the plane.

"Sorry," she silently mouths to them before turning her attention back to me, her voice a hushed whisper-shout, "How in the world is it that you don't like ice cream?"

"I have no reason. I don't," I reply calmly, relishing how her eyes widen with each word. I wonder if she'd look like that when on her knees.... Okay, don't go there, Alex. The last thing I need is to sport a bulge right here, in front of everyone.

"That isn't right. You've got to try one once we get to New York. I'm sure they have a lot of amazing ice cream places," she suggests, stifling a yawn as exhaustion takes its toll.

"Yeah, but right now, you need to get some sleep, or you'll faint before we get to one," I advise, observing how her eyes struggle to stay o pen.

"Okay," she mumbles, rising from her seat and heading to the inner room of the plane.

Glancing down at my laptop, I notice an unopened email from the prince. "Okay, let's see what this is about."

Chapter 15

Olivia

"Don't we have something to talk about?" I ask, my gaze fixed on Alex's impassive face.

"I don't think so," he replies calmly, his voice cold and detached.

"Okay," I say, setting his cup of coffee on his desk before leaving his office. Tears threaten to spill from my eyes, but I refuse to let them fall, blinking rapidly and pushing them back.

I had hoped we could discuss the kiss just as Richard suggested to find out how he feels about me. But I chickened out at the last minute, terrified of hearing an answer I didn't want.

I didn't ask for this. I didn't ask to be enthralled by Alex. There's no better way to put it. Every spare moment, my thoughts are consumed by him.

I try not to think of him, especially at work, but I can't stop myself. Images flood my mind. Alex pressed against me, my back against the door, his blue eyes darkened with desire as they roamed over me.

The way he claimed I drove him wild, the possessive way he called me his. Thoughts of him haunt me at work, and when I lay my head down at night, he invades my dreams.

I've done everything I could to push aside the uncomfortable heat that lingers on my skin, to suppress the memories of that kiss from last week and the way we fit together so perfectly.

Sitting up straight, I rest my fingertips on the edge of my desk. The feelings I have for Alexander McQueen can't be denied. Emotions swirl within me every time I think of him, each time a different storm of emotions.

I now wonder what might have happened if I hadn't pushed him away. If I had stayed in his office and surrendered to the forbidden desires he ignites within me. Suppose I had stayed in his office and stripped for him. What would he have done?

And more importantly, what would I have done?

I've been replaying that scene in my mind for the past week, in every quiet moment, whenever his office door comes into view—the scenario where I stay, where I'm bold and let my desires rule.

But then, the doubts and complications surge back. What would Camila say? How would Abel feel? Is it worth risking my relationship with my best friend and brother for this intoxicating but dangerous attraction?

Also, I couldn't help but acknowledge the burning ache in my heart. It gnaws at me that he hadn't even brought up our kiss. Instead, he had gone to great lengths to avoid me since that moment. Did my kiss repel him so much that he couldn't bear to face me?

No, that couldn't be it. I vividly recall the sensation of his hard, substantial bulge pressing against my stomach during that heated kiss.

He had reveled in it; there was no doubt in my mind. He chose to act like an insufferable jerk.

A sudden surge of anger courses through me, a fiery rage at his audacity to evade discussing the kiss as if it had never happened. My blood boils even hotter at the realization that he had managed to get away with it, all because I allowed him to.

"You could have told me we were going to New York tonight. I could have been more prepared," I grumble sourly beside Alexander as we walk towards his private plane.

After regular working hours, he summoned me into his office and casually dropped the bombshell that we had to fly out to New York on short notice. Who, in their right mind, springs such a last-minute trip on someone? My boss.

My mood darkened even further when I realized I had forgotten to pack my tampons. It was terrible timing, with my period looming on the horizon. I could only hope it wouldn't make an untimely appearance during our stay in New York, though that seemed wishful thinking.

At the very least, I prayed it wouldn't put me in an embarrassing situation. I mentally crossed my fingers, hoping for that small mercy.

"Well, if I had been aware of this, I would have informed you earlier. You're not the only one inconvenienced by this," He snaps, looking irritated.

"Although I guess this wouldn't be inconvenient for you, considering your excitement." He adds dryly as he gets into the plane.

As we settle into the plane, Alex wastes no time and brings out his laptop, its keyboard clacking away. It's as though this man's entire existence revolves around work.

After stowing my luggage, I approach him cautiously. "Is there anything I can do?" I inquire calmly, my voice soft.

He lifts his gaze slowly from the laptop, his eyes sweeping over me in a way that sends a warm flush through my body, making my head feel light.

"No, there's not. You can rest. It's a long flight ahead," his husky voice replies before he returns to his work.

I nod softly, though a tinge of sadness creeps in at the realization that he doesn't need my assistance. I settle into a seat in front of him, berating myself inwardly. How pathetic can you be, Olivia?

"There are other seats in the plane," he points out, fingers never pausing their dance on the keyboard. What is he so engrossed in?

With a casual shrug, I respond, "Yeah, I know. I want to sit here, just in case you might need anything. Is there a problem with that?" It's a bold move, a tone I've never used with him before. I wonder how he'll react.

He remains silent but arches an eyebrow, tilting his head to the side as he studies me. I meet his gaze with a forced smile, anticipation hanging heavy in the air.

His expression remains impassive, lips pressed tightly together. His hair neatly gelled back, reveals a streak of silver.

After a lingering moment of silence, he finally concedes, "Okay, you can stay here," and returns to the damn incessant clicking of his laptop.

An unbidden yawn escapes my mouth, and I hastily try to stifle it with my hands.

From across the seat, Alex's body vibrates with laughter. "Trying to swallow me whole or what?" he teases, a smirk on his lips.

"I wasn't that loud!" I protest, feeling embarrassed that he witnessed my moment of vulnerability.

"Sure," he replies, his tongue lightly pressed against his cheek.

"I wasn't loud!" I assert, my defense tinged with wounded pride.

Cocking an eyebrow at me, he retorts cheekily, "I didn't say a word."

"You didn't have to. It's written all over your face," I mutter, sinking into the chair, my hair falling over my face.

I've been in this seat for the past hour, watching Alex work. He wasn't kidding when he said he didn't need my help. He's been glued to his chair, typing away without a break, not even a trip to the restroom. I was bored but didn't expect my yawn to be so audible.

"If anything, you look cute when you yawn," he says with a playful grin.

Clearing my throat, I whisper, feeling my cheeks flush with heat, "Thank you."

We fall into a comfortable silence when suddenly, he breaks it with a question, "What are your allergies?"

"Allergies?" I ask, my face contorted in confusion.

"Yes, allergies," he confirms. "We'll be staying at a hotel where meals will be served, so I need to know if you have any allergies. That way, they can accommodate your dietary restrictions."

"Oh," I respond, the realization dawning.

"Well?" He prompts.

"I'm allergic to peanut butter, and while I'm not allergic to tomatoes, I don't particularly like them," I say.

"Tomatoes?" He asks, his surprise evident in his tone.

"Why?" He asks, eyebrows shooting upwards.

I can't fathom why people react so strongly when I mention my dislike for tomatoes. I get it; many people adore them, but I don't. That's also why I wouldn't say I like burgers with all those mushy tomatoes– yuck.

I shrug and explain, "I don't know, they just seem so mushy and gross," my mouth twisting with distaste at the thought.

"And here, I thought I was the weird one for not liking ice cream," he mutters quietly, but I hear it.

"You don't like ice cream," I exclaim, my outburst drawing curious glances from him and a few of Alex's business associates aboard the plane.

"Sorry," I silently mouth them before turning my attention back to him, my voice now a hushed whisper-shout, "How in the world can you not like ice cream?"

"I have no reason. I don't," he replies calmly, shrugging lightly.

"That's just not right. You have to try some once we get to New York. I'm sure they have plenty of amazing ice cream places," I suggest, stifling a yawn. My mind races through all the different flavors he should try classic vanilla, rich chocolate chip, refreshing mint chocolate chip, and sweet strawberry. There are so many delicious options.

"Yeah, but right now, you need to get some sleep, or you'll faint before we get to one," he says, his gaze fixed on me.

He's right. I can barely keep my eyes open, feeling them fluttering shut.

"Okay," I mumble, rising from my seat and heading to the inner room of the plane.

Pushing a door open and stumbling into a room, I stare in awe, my mouth wide open. A fly can enter, and I probably won't even feel it.

The room's interior exudes luxury and sophistication, a sanctuary amidst the clouds. The walls are paneled with rich, dark wood, adorned with subtle golden accents that catch the soft, warm glow of concealed lighting. Plush, cream-colored leather seats offer a luxurious contrast to the dark wood, their ergonomic design ensuring both comfort and style.

Large, tinted windows stretch along the length of the cabin, allowing the gentle caress of sunlight to filter in, illuminating the house in a soft, ethereal glow. Heavy curtains hang beside each window, ready to be drawn for those seeking privacy or to block out the outside world.

The cabin's centerpiece is a gleaming mahogany table, perfectly polished and adorned with an elegant floral arrangement. Crystal glasses and delicate china are carefully set, promising an exquisite dining experience in the sky.

Overhead, the ceiling boasts a constellation of tiny, twinkling lights that mimic a starry night. The enchanting effect creates a sense of tranquility, making it easy to forget the bustling world below.

It is a room that whispers of comfort and luxury. I know Alex is rich, but just how rich is he?

"Wow," I exclaim aloud, my voice filled with amazement as I step gently onto the plush carpet that leads to the queen-sized bed at the center of the room.

Sitting down on the edge of the bed, I reach out and run my hand over the silky texture of the sheets, giving in to the urge to bounce lightly on the mattress. It's far more comfortable than the bed back in my apartment. This room is more significant than my entire apartment.

My fingers grasp a pillow encased in a silk pillowcase, and I draw it closer, pressing my head into its softness. "Ah, so soft," I sigh with pleasure. "Just for a little while, I'll sleep, just. For. A. Little. While," I mumble sleepily, my eyes fluttering shut.

Chapter 16

Alexander

"What the hell do I pay you for then?" I bellow into the phone, my frustration boiling over.

"I'm, I..."The voice on the other end stammers, its words disintegrating into incoherence.

Where on earth did I find these dimwits?

"I don't care how you do it, just fix it, or you lose your job!" I declare firmly, abruptly ending the call.

That marks the fourth call in the past 10 minutes. I can't fathom why these individuals hold positions of power and authority in their respective offices when they can't execute a simple task.

"Phew, you should calm yourself down. You wouldn't want to arrive all riled up at the meeting," Daniel suggests as he carefully places a glass of whiskey before me.

Downing the entire glass at once, I savor the fiery trail it leaves in my chest.

"Trust me, I am calm," I declare, my fingers instinctively tightening around the now-empty whiskey glass.

"Sure," he replies, his attention fixed on the tablet resting on his thighs. "There's a storm brewing, so we'll arrive in New York late."

"Exactly what I needed," I grumble softly, the words slipping beneath my breath.

"You should go rest. You've been working non-stop for the past four hours," he suggests, his gaze finally lifting to meet mine.

A mischievous smile tugs at my lips. "Are you worried about me, Daniel?" I tease, the question wrapped in a playful tone.

He responds with a flat, matter-of-fact tone. "No. You won't be useful to anybody if you end up dead from overexerting yourself with work."

"Whatever," I scoff, feigning indifference.

As I gaze up at Daniel, a peculiar notion strikes me, one so absurd that it gives me pause before I finally voice it.

"Is there a reason you're attempting to bore a hole into my face with that stare?" He asks, his words laced with a hint of uncertainty.

He doesn't lift his eyes from his tablet. "What would you do if you liked someone, but that person is strictly off-limits?" I inquire, my gaze locked on him as he slowly raises his head to meet my eyes.

A chuckle escapes his lips, a sound that feels unexpected and out of place. "This is interesting, really interesting," he laughs.

Perplexed, I press for clarification. "What do you mean?" I query.

He meets my inquiry with a playful, toothy grin. "Finally, someone's managed to crack through that ice around your heart," he remarks.

Frustration wells within me, and I pour another glass of whiskey. Why have I even bothered to ask him? Daniel has a knack for exploiting and holding my vulnerabilities over my head. He does it for fun, but it doesn't kill the urge to smash his head, for fun too.

"Is it Olivia?" he suddenly probes, causing me to sputter and cough, whiskey escaping from my mouth in surprise.

Wiping my mouth with a napkin, I attempt to maintain composure. "I have no idea what you're talking about," I reply, my heart racing.

I trust Daniel, but his uncanny ability to discern my thoughts makes me wonder if I'm being too obvious. Can others easily see through me, or is he simply an astute observer?

"You don't fool me, Alex," he asserts, his countenance void of fun as he sets aside his tablet. "I've observed how you regard her, even when her eyes are elsewhere. It's a look that venerates her as if she were life incarnate, the very nucleus of your universe. You peer at her like the boundless galaxies, and your affection extends to each star within." His words resonate with a tender sincerity.

I swallow hard, my fingers instinctively tugging at my tie. "You think you've got me all figured out, huh?" I respond, my lips pressed into a thin line.

He chuckles softly and replies, "Well, of course. We've known each other for the past decade, after all. Who else would be able to see through all your bullshit?"

"Yeah," I laugh while sinking into the plush leather chair.

"So, what's the problem? Why aren't you going after what's clearly in your heart?" he prods.

"It's not as simple as it may seem," I reply, the weight of my thoughts evident in a heavy sigh, followed by another sip of my drink.

"Is it because of her brother? Abel?" He dismisses it with a scoff. "He'll come around. And Camila? Camila adores you, and I'm certain she'd support whatever brings you happiness," he insists.

But he's overlooking a vital detail.

"Or is it because of that incident?" He asks with a wry tilt of his head.

I nod in agreement.

The incident that transpired 25 years ago is an indelible scar that continues to haunt my memories and taint every fiber of my being.

"It's been 25 years, Alex. It's time to move on. No one would hold that against you," he implores, his voice laced with exasperation.

Rising to my full height, I utter, "That's the thing. I hold it against myself."

With purpose in my steps, I make my way to my room. There, I shed my jacket, loosen my tie, and roll up my sleeves, the weariness in my eyes a testament to the hours spent hunched over that relentless laptop.

Taking a right turn, my keen eye catches sight of a partially open door. I approach it with quiet grace and discover Olivia sprawled haphazardly on the bed, drawing a brief, subdued laugh from me.

I should turn away. I should shut her door all the way and go to my room.

But I don't.

Instead, my legs find their way into her room, my eyes watching her sleep. It's creepy, even for me. But I don't stop. I can't.

She's so pretty when she thinks no one is watching. Dark circles are forming under her eyes from working so late and hard these days. I feel a sharp twinge of guilt.

I want to smooth them away, to bring them back again. But I want her to be tired from staying up all night, ravaged by my desire, until she's depleted of all her strength. Even then, I'll still do her.

Blinking my eyes rapidly and looking up at the ceiling, I feel my chest expand with desires.

Moving closer to her, I notice she still has her heels on. She must have been so tired not even to take them off.

I take the heel of her leg in my hand and take the heels off as gently as I can. They make a soft thud as they hit the plush carpet.

Olivia mumbles in her sleep as she turns around in the bed and raises a leg, exposing her luscious thighs...and the end of my composure.

Her rosy nipples press against the thin material of her silk blouse, and my mouth waters with the need to take one into my mouth and suck on it until she's wriggling beneath me.

I lick my lips.

Her tantalizing olive skin is on full display as her lacy pants stare right at me. My member hardens. I close my eyes and take a slow, deep breath, working to regain control.

Just lay the covers on her and leave. I think to myself.

"Alex," she mumbles my name from sleep, a small moan escaping her lips.

Cursing softly, I leave the room, turning off the air conditioning.

I couldn't sleep.

I had collapsed into bed two hours ago, my body exhausted, but my mind was racing like I had injected it with a dozen espresso shots.

I tried counting sheep, a secret habit that had always helped me fall asleep. I thought about how this vast deal would benefit my company in a big way. I tried listening to my alarm clock's built-in white noise feature, but nothing worked.

Images of Olivia's red lacy panties play on the screen of my mind's eye; whenever I close my eyes, it's like a broken loop.

I groan and turn on my side, hoping the change in position would shake the persistent memory of Olivia moaning my name in her sleep.

It doesn't.

Chapter 17

Olivia

My eyes feel scratchy as I force them open. Thankfully, the room is cloaked in darkness, sparing me from the relentless morning sunlight trying to invade through the window.

With a groan, I roll over in bed, my fingers brushing against the smooth silk pillowcase. "Mmm... nothing quite like silk," I mumble contentedly.

Silk? But my pillows at home are encased in cotton.

Oh, dear Lord.

Suddenly, I bolt upright, my drowsiness vanishing in an instant. My eyes dart around, taking in the unfamiliar surroundings—the grandeur of the king-sized bed and the full-length mirror beside it. I stare at my reflection through the mirror, my messy hair sticking out in all directions, a little drool glistening on my chin.

My gaze falls upon the wall clock above the mirror, and I gasp in horror.

"Shit, shit!" I mutter in a panicked frenzy as I hastily leap out of bed, my toe colliding with the bed's sturdy leg. "Damn it!" I groan, clutching my throbbing toe, pain mingling with my rising confusion and anxiety.

Suddenly, the memories come surging back with unrelenting force. Alex mentioned our trip to New York, my reluctant complaints, the journey aboard his private plane, and finally, arriving in this room and surrendering to sleep.

Damn.

I'm heading to New York!

Hurrying to the window shrouded in heavy curtains, I pull them aside slightly, my eyes locking onto the expanse of clouds in the sky.

Holy shit.

Hurriedly, I enter the bathroom, my whole being vibrating with an electrifying excitement as I fully absorb the reality that I'm embarking on a journey to a city I've always yearned to explore.

Yesterday, I didn't quite have the time to grasp the magnitude of going to New York, but right now? I can feel my senses tingling with anticipation.

I quickly brush my teeth, wash my face, and then slip into a white button-down shirt, a sleek black skirt, and a pair of pumps. My fingers rush through my hair, hastily securing it into a ponytail.

The image of Alex bending to remove my shoes suddenly flashes before me. What the hell was that about?

I shake my head, trying to clear the unexpected memory, then walk over to the mirror and give my flushed cheeks a reassuring pat. Nodding to my reflection, I utter, "You've got this," before striding out of the room.

"Nice of you to join us," Alex says dryly, his fingers dancing across his phone screen, reclining against the pristine white couch, one leg casually crossing the other.

He's dressed in a sharp, navy blue suit, a striking complement to his sun-kissed skin. Today, his usually slicked-back brown hair remains untouched, forming a cascade of elegant curls atop his head. It might have appeared chaotic to anyone else, but on Alexander, it seems divine, framing his face with effortless perfection.

I stammer, my cheeks flushing with embarrassment. "I'm sorry I woke up late."

"It's fine," he retorts sharply, pushing himself up from the couch and striding past me. His after-shave scent envelops my senses, and I am momentarily lost in the lingering fragrance. "We're here."

The frigid air hits my face like a thousand icy needles as we disembark from the plane. Immediately, I notice a ring of ten stern-faced security guards encircling us.

"We've been expecting you, Mr. McQueen," a tall, burly man with hair that dances wildly in the unforgiving wind says to Alex, his voice carrying the weight of authority and anticipation.

"It's nice to meet you," Daniel, Alex's lawyer, says with a subtle smile, extending his hand to the man politely.

I observe their handshake briefly before my attention is drawn elsewhere. "Come on," the man, whom I now recognize as Ryan, thanks to the name tag on his uniform, ushers us from the plane toward a waiting car.

"Stop shaking your leg," Alex snaps, his tone cutting through the air like a blade. My hands immediately reach my knees, desperately trying to quell the involuntary trembling. "Sorry," I mumble, the word slipping out almost like an apology to my nerves.

But I can't help it. It's my first time in this unfamiliar city, and anxiety courses through me like an electric current. The restless movement of my legs is a reflex, a physical manifestation of my unease.

Suddenly, Alex's hand descends firmly onto my knee, holding me in place. I can feel the warmth emanating from his touch, a tingling sensation that sends a shiver up my spine. I sneak a sidelong glance at him, only to find his attention consumed by his phone. His jaw is clenched, his brows furrowed, and I'm left wondering what I had expected from this situation.

Did I foolishly hope for him to be captivated by my presence? My subconscious sneers in silent mockery, reminding me of the futility of such daydreams.

The car comes to an abrupt halt, jolting me from my thoughts. I peer out the window, only to find us parked in front of an inviting ice cream shop.

"Come on. You mentioned wanting me to try some ice cream, right?" Alex's gaze fixes on me, his eyes holding a hint of playful challenge.

I stammer in response, caught off guard by his commitment to my passing remark. "Yeah, I mean, but I, uh... I didn't think you'd go through with it."

It had been a casual comment, something I blurted out in the heat of the moment. That he's taken it to heart warms me in a way I hadn't expected.

"Well, we're here now, aren't we? Come on out," he urges as he exits the car.

Gathering my bag, I follow suit, leaving the driver behind in the vehicle. Daniel, his lawyer, had already prepared for the impending deal, going with a chauffeur to explore the city at our leisure.

The quaint Ice cream shop stands on the corner of a busy street, its pastel-colored façade a delightful contrast against the azure sky. The inviting aroma of freshly baked waffle cones wafts through the air, luring passersby with promises of sweet indulgence.

As we step inside, the door makes a ding sound, heading straight to the counter.

A vibrant array of frozen delights beckons through the large, crystal-clear windows in ornate glass cases. Each flavor glistens under the soft, golden glow of pendant lights, casting an enchanting aura upon the rows of frozen treasures.

"Is there anything I can get you, sir?" The waiter inquires, her voice tinged with a hint of sultriness. She's a young woman, perhaps a year younger than myself, and her unabashed gaze is fixed on Alex.

Her eyes wander his form suggestively, and she leans provocatively against the counter, her white cut-out top accentuating her already exposed cleavage.

I can feel my jaw clench involuntarily as I contemplate suggesting to Alex that we find another place for our ice cream or perhaps even abandon the idea altogether.

But Alex's voice breaks through, snapping me out of my silent staring contest with the waiter, who appears solely fixated on him. "What do you think?" he asks, his eyes shifting to meet mine.

I stammered, caught off guard. "Uh?" I mumble before regaining my composure.

"Which flavor should I get?" He fixes me with an intent gaze, waiting for my recommendation.

"Oh, uhm..." I clear my throat, trying to focus. "You should have the mint chocolate chip; it's perfect," I suggest.

"Okay," he nods and turns to the waiter, who's still standing there with an air of sensuality. "I'll have that."

"Of course," she purrs in response before sensually strutting away, leaving me to wrestle with my unease.

We go to a secluded corner at the back of the ice cream shop, finding a relatively empty spot. We've barely settled into our seats when our order arrives.

"One vanilla ice cream for you," the waiter announces, placing the cone in front of me.

"And one mint chocolate for the gentleman here," she adds seductively, setting Alex's ice cream before him.

"Thank you," Alex responds curtly, his attention not wavering from the tempting mint chocolate swirls.

I can't help but feel a strange satisfaction as I notice the disappointment wash over the waiter's face.

"Well, if you need anything, you can just call for me," she offers, her gaze locked on Alex, waiting for his acknowledgment.

But he remains silent, focusing solely on the mint chocolate cone, his hands gently swirling the cone.

"Thank you," I mutter, mustering a forced smile as she huffs and retreats, leaving us to enjoy our ice cream in peace.

"It's going to melt if you keep staring at it like you're staring at a document you can't seem to understand," I quip, my gaze shifting from the ice cream to Alex. He's been fixated on it for a few minutes, his face an enigmatic mask.

"Come on, try it," I urge, attempting to pull him from his contemplation.

He sighs, finally relenting, and picks up the spoon from the table. With reluctance, he scoops a portion and takes a bite.

I watch intently as he savors the flavor, his tongue darting out to taste the creamy goodness.

"So, how was it?" I ask eagerly, anticipation in my voice.

"It tastes like toothpaste," he replies, his tone flat.

"What? That's not possible," I mumble, shocked by his reaction. I had expected a much more positive response.

He shrugs. "That's how it tastes."

Determined to prove him wrong, I grab his cone and take a scoop myself. "Let me see," I mumble, my taste buds tingling with anticipation. After a bite, I can't help but exclaim, "This is so good!" Taking another scoop, I point the spoon at his ice cream. "Your taste buds are whack."

"I want yours," he says, nodding toward my half-eaten ice cream.

"All right," I agree, sliding it over to him across the table. But I pause momentarily, adding with a playful tone, "I don't want to hear you slandering this one as well. If you do, I'm charging you with a crime."

"Which crime?" he chuckles.

"For disrespecting ice cream. It's a serious offense," I declare with mock solemnity.

"Oh, really now?" he teases.

"Yup," I affirm, emphasizing the 'P' as I speak.

I watch as he takes a scoop of my vanilla ice cream. "Hmmmm..." he nods appreciatively, savoring the flavor. "Now, this," he points to the ice cream, "might just be my favorite."

I giggle softly, teasing him, "You've only tried two flavors. I doubt it'll still be your favorite once you've tasted the others."

He shakes his head with conviction. "Nope, I know this is it. No other flavors can compare to this," he insists, taking another generous scoop.

Who would have thought I'd find myself in an ice cream shop in another city, sharing ice cream with Alex, my boss? His relaxed demeanor and genuine smile contrast the permanent scowl he usually wears. Seeing him enjoying himself and genuinely having a good time is refreshing. I suppose a little time away from the legalities of the trip and business was exactly what he needed after a long flight.

As he indulges in the ice cream, I can't help but imagine an alternate life, one where we're just co-workers casually hanging out at an ice cream shop, talking and enjoying each other's company without the complications of our relationships with Abel and Camila.

In that fleeting moment, it's just him and me, sitting in an ice cream shop, savoring our treats in comfortable silence.

"I want more. Can I have more?" Alex looks up, a hint of ice cream clinging to the corner of his chin.

Suppressing a laugh, I point to his face and say, "You've got something there."

His hands attempt to locate the ice cream, but he misses it entirely. "Where?" he asks, genuinely puzzled.

"Hold on," I say, reaching for a napkin and leaning over the table to clean his chin.

"That's it," I murmur, my gaze meeting his. With my chest close to his face, I feel a sudden vulnerability in this intimate proximity. The hunger in his dark blue eyes weakens my legs, and we find ourselves locked in a silent, intense gaze.

Just as things seem to be taking an unexpected turn, a voice shatters the moment. "This is your bill," the same waiter from earlier says, her expression sour as she breaks the silence.

Chapter 18

Alexander

"What do you mean there's only one room left?" I exclaim, my bewilderment tinged with frustration.

"I'm so sorry, sir. Due to the bad weather, the hotel was overbooked, and we only have one room left for you," the receptionist apologizes.

I snap, my tone sharp and angry, "I don't need your damn apology! Two rooms were reserved since yesterday, and you're telling me this now?"

"Isn't there anything you can do?" Olivia asks softly from beside me.

"I'm sorry, ma'am," the receptionist shakes her head.

Taking out my cell phone from my suit, I dial Daniel's number. It rings twice before he picks up, "Mind telling me why there's only one room booked here?" I ask.

"What?" He grunts, his voice disoriented over the phone.

"Are you seriously sleeping right now?" I scoff.

"Well, technically," he yawns, "I was sleeping before you called me. What's going on?"

Biting my tongue, unwilling to cause a scene here, I calmly say, "The hotel you booked has only one room available. Book another hotel".

"I can't", he says.

"What?" I ask, incredulous.

"I can't," he repeats, matter-of-factly, "There's a huge storm coming, so all the other hotels are fully booked. I'm sure it was an oversight from their end to have only one room available for you given that was your usual booking", he says.

Sighing deeply, I clench my teeth. I've never been the one to think of murder, but right now, I'm so damn close to killing him.

"But, think of the bright side. You and Olivia get to spend the night together..."

He adds, laughing.

"That fucker," I mutter, my voice carrying a simmering frustration as I hang up the phone.

Turning to Olivia, I ask, "Do you mind sleeping in the same room? It's just for tonight. First thing tomorrow morning, I'll get us another hotel." I shoot a withering glare at the receptionist before continuing, "One where they're competent enough." My words drip with disdain as I voice my discontent with the current situation.

"It's not a problem, Sir," she responds softly.

I sigh gently, shifting my focus toward the receptionist. "Lead us to our room."

"Breakfast is available at 7 am. We trust you'll have a pleasant stay," she adds with a gracious bow before gracefully exiting the room.

"Wow," Olivia murmurs, her eyes absorbing every intricate detail of the room.

Soft, muted lighting cast a warm, golden glow, bathing the space in an inviting ambiance. The king-sized bed is draped in silky sheets of the palest ivory. It's so feminine.

"There's only one bed," Olivia remarks, her gaze fixated on the lone bed occupying the room's center.

I sigh in relief as I spot a couch beside the dressing mirror. It's a curious touch, reminiscent of a bygone era, a rarity in modern hotel rooms. Daniel is going to hear it from me.

"I'll take the couch. You can have the bed," I propose, placing my leather briefcase on the brown upholstery and smoothly removing my blazer.

"What? No, you're paying for the room; you should take the bed, Sir," Olivia insists, her eyes widening slightly in protest.

"It's Alex," I snapped tersely.

"What?" She responds, her curiosity piqued.

I loosen my tie, unbuttoning a few upper buttons on my shirt as I approach her. Her eyes widen, torn between meeting my gaze and stealing glances at the patch of skin exposed on my chest.

"It's Alex," I emphasize firmly. "Since we left the ice cream shop, you've been addressing me as 'Sir,' and it's beginning to get on my nerves," I admit, clenching my jaw with frustration.

"Okay," she whispers.

"Okay, what?" I inquire, raising an eyebrow.

"Okay, Alex," she responds, nodding.

"Good," I acknowledge, swiftly shedding my shirt smoothly.

"Oh my God!" Olivia gasped, her hands instinctively flying to cover her face. "What are you doing? Why are you taking off your shirt?" Her voice quivers with astonishment.

Chuckling deeply, thoroughly charmed by her innocence, I explain, "I'm just going to the bathroom to shower, sweetheart. You can change while I'm gone."

After a quick, rejuvenating hot shower, I rummage through the closet, finding blankets to make the hotel couch more comfortable. At least the place isn't entirely useless.

Once I'm done, Olivia takes her turn to freshen up, emerging from the bathroom in a cozy two-piece cotton pajama set. She looks adorable, but I can sense her embarrassment. I reassure her that there's no reason to be embarrassed.

Now, we lie in silence. She's on the bed, and I've settled onto the couch. The room is quiet, with only the gentle hum of the air conditioning breaking the stillness.

"Did you ever think about what you would have become if you weren't a CEO?" Olivia's question cuts through the hush.

My gaze drifts toward her, tucked under the blankets, her hair splayed across the pillow.

Clearing my throat, I reply, "I probably would have become a chef."

"A chef?" She sounds surprised.

"Yeah," I confirm with a soft smile. "I've always loved cooking since I was a child. I remember spending time in the kitchen with my mom, learning different recipes and helping her while the other boys played football in the fields. I had few friends because they all saw me as a Mama's boy. They even tried to bully me over it, but Abel beat the crap out of them, even if we were only five years old," I reminisce, fondly recalling the memory.

Olivia giggles softly, "That's interesting. I would have never thought my brother to be the violent type."

"Oh, he wasn't, except on rare occasions," I clarify.

"Yeah, I guess," she replies, stifling a yawn.

Silence descends once more.

A pause in the moment.

"How about you? What would you have become if you weren't my assistant?" I ask.

There's no immediate response.

"Olivia?" I call out her name in the dimly lit room.

Suddenly, I hear her snoring softly.

A smile graces my lips as I rest my forearm over my eyes.

"Goodnight," I whisper into the stillness of the room.

Chapter 19

Olivia

"Wake up," a voice insists, accompanied by an insistent hand shaking my shoulder.

Groaning, I swat my hands away and turn onto my stomach, clutching the soft pillow to my head.

A deep, masculine chuckle reaches my ears. I must be dreaming. Today is supposed to be the day I pick up Irene's birthday gift. I'll get to that as soon as I wake up.

"If you don't get up now, you're gonna get fired," the voice warns again, sounding distant.

"Just need one more minute," I mumble, raising my index finger as a sign of delay.

Wait, fired?

I jolt awake, sitting up abruptly and inadvertently smacking my hands against the wall. "Ow!" I hear a pained voice, and I see Alex standing there, his palm pressed to his forehead, eyes tightly shut, and a wince on his face.

My eyes widen in realization. Oh my God. I didn't hit the wall. And today isn't Irene's birthday.

I hit my boss square on the forehead after he tried to wake me up.

Shit!

"I am so sorry!" I exclaimed, rushing out of bed to stand in front of him. "Can I see?" I ask, my voice quiet with concern.

Alex slowly opens his eyes and lowers his hands, revealing an angry red mark on his forehead.

"Oh no," I gasp, covering my mouth with my hand. This is bad, no, this is horrible. He has every right to fire me after this.

Gently pressing my finger against his throbbing forehead, I wince at his sharp intake of breath. "Let me get some ice for that," I suggest. "Come, sit here." I guide him to the chair in front of the dressing table, which I've turned sideways to facilitate our makeshift first aid.

I quickly grabbed a plastic bag from my luggage, dropped some ice from the fridge, and rushed back to him, forgetting to grab a washcloth to envelop it. "This is going to be cold," I warn as I apply the cold pack to his forehead.

"Ya think?" he returns gruffly.

I firmly press it against his injured skin and contemplate other job options. After what I've just done, I'm unsure if I'll still have a job to return to.

I could contact Patty; she might still give me a job. Patty always seemed to adore me, or so I thought. Then again, I did disappear without a word. Another possibility is the department store, but I recall slapping our manager for grabbing me inappropriately. I doubt they'd even allow me through the mall's entrance.

"You're going to make your lips bleed if you continue biting them," Alex remarks dryly, his eyes closed as I tend to his injury.

I immediately withdraw my bottom lip from between my teeth. It's a habit I'm addicted to, one I indulge in when I'm anxious, nervous, or embarrassed. Right now, I'm feeling all three emotions simultaneously.

"Sorry," I mumble softly, my remorse evident in my tone.

"Come here," he grunts, pulling me onto his lap, our bodies arranged sideways, with my hands instinctively finding purchase on his shoulders.

"Uh," I stammer, afraid to form a coherent sentence. His firm hands on my hips send a palpable heat coursing through my skin, through the fabric of my pajamas.

Clearing my throat, attempting to regain my composure, I finally ask, "What are you doing?" My voice quivers, and I mentally wince at how shaky my voice sounds.

"I know what you're thinking, but it's not going to happen," he asserts firmly. "I won't fire you, but you will be punished."

"Punished?" I whisper, my voice barely audible.

"Yes, punished," he says huskily, his grip on my hips intensifying. My breath becomes shallow as we lock eyes, my gaze sliding from his face to his lips. I wonder if we're both thinking the same thing, if he's contemplating the same kiss that's crossed my mind.

The friction between us serves up an enticing catalyst or segue way.

"Get dressed. You have twenty minutes," he instructs, setting me gently on my feet before abruptly leaving the room, leaving me hanging, feeling a mixture of emotions and drenched below.

"Oh God," I exhale, my eyes falling to the now unfrozen ice pack in my hands, water droplets seeping onto the wooden floor.

"It's a pleasure to meet you, Your Highness," Alex says, extending his hand with respect. He exchanges a firm handshake with the man before him, who stands tall despite his relatively young age and exudes an air of quiet intimidation.

His attire speaks of untold wealth and refinement, with a robe of rich silk and intricate embroidery adorned with the finest jewels that glistened like distant stars against the dark expanse of the Arabian night. A Kaffiyeh rests upon his head, its white fabric contrasting with his bronzed complexion, and its edges held in place by a gleaming Agal.

His piercing, ebony eyes are set on Alex, and his firm, chiseled features hint at a lineage steeped in history. His beard, neatly trimmed, frames a mouth that quickly curls up into a smile.

"I am glad we finally get the chance to have this meeting," he says, his Arabian accent seeping through. "Come on, let's go in," he adds.

They enter the conference room – Alex, Daniel, and the Arabian prince. I, on the other hand, am left outside. Even the prince's entourage remains in the hallway. It seems that the prince values his privacy regarding business matters. Well, that only gives me more time to explore this intriguing restaurant.

As I wander through the elegant establishment, savoring the ambiance and décor, Daniel's excited voice pierces through my thoughts. I hastily set down my second glass of margarita and rushed towards them.

"Did it go well?" I inquired, eager to learn the outcome of their meeting.

"Yeah, it did!" Daniel exclaims, his face illuminated by an exuberant grin, while Alex offers a more reserved but contented smile.

"That's great news. Why don't—" I begin to suggest, but the embarrassing roar of my stomach interrupts me. Oh no! I close my eyes in mortification as I hear Alexander and Daniel burst into amused laughter.

"That wasn't my stomach," I declare, attempting to save face.

"Yeah, no, it wasn't," Alexander says, shaking his head, a faint smile lingering on his lips.

I press my lips together, determined to salvage the situation. "I'm sure you must be famished. Why don't we get something to eat?" I propose, offering a tight smile.

"Of course," Alex chuckles, "before your stomach swallows us all." He shares a laugh with Daniel as they continue ahead.

"It wasn't my stomach!" I protest once more, drawing a few curious glances from nearby diners.

Chapter 20

Alexander

"You look like you're about to piss yourself," Daniel says from beside me, his eyes dancing with amusement.

"Shut up," I snap, my nerves making my tone sharper than I intended.

"Relax, she's not gonna run for the hills once she sees you, oh, eagerly waiting for her in the hallway of her hotel floor," he adds, his teasing tone unmistakable.

I turn sharply toward him, a mixture of irritation and anxiety in my gaze. "What are you even doing here?"

"What do you mean?" He shrugs. "It's a dinner to celebrate the deal we closed, right? I have the right to be here," he grins, seemingly enjoying my discomfort.

"Daniel," I say his name with a warning tone.

"What?" He snorts, shoving his hands deeper into his pants pockets.

"I thought you had plans," I say through gritted teeth.

"I do?" He asks, feigning innocence. "Wow, I wasn't aware," he says, his smile widening.

Unfolding my arms, I'm about to snap at him when a soft voice stops me, "Hi!"

Turning around, I see Olivia in the dress I had specially chosen for her, and my breath catches in my throat.

The elegant dinner gown drapes gracefully over her curvy form, accentuating every curve with finesse. Its deep, crimson-colored fabric shimmers softly under the ambient lights in the hotel room, casting an alluring glow upon her. The gown features an off-shoulder neckline, showcasing her shoulders and collarbone while delicately framing her décolletage.

The gown's fitted bodice hugs her hourglass silhouette, cinching at the waist before cascading into a flowing, A-line skirt that gracefully brushes the floor as she walks toward me. It seems time has stopped now, and I can only see Olivia.

"Hi," she breathes again, her red-coated lips entrancing me like a love potion.

"You look wonderful," I choke out, my voice barely above a whisper.

"Thank you," she says, a faint blush on her cheeks.

"Oh, it's nice to see you too, Daniel," she adds, smiling at my nemesis beside me.

"It's nice to see you too, Olivia. You look stunning," he adds a little smile.

"Aren't you leaving?" I ask Daniel, my eyebrows cocked, hoping he would take the hint. He looks at me, a grin on his face, and for a moment, I think he's about to do or say something ridiculous, although I wouldn't put it past him.

"Sure," he nods, his grin undeterred. "I will see you guys tomorrow. I have plans, you see."

"Oh," Olivia says, her expression changing slightly as we both watch my lawyer's lanky form walk down the hall.

"Good evening. Let me lead you to your table, please," the waiter greets with a pleasant smile as she escorts us to our table in the luxurious restaurant I had reserved for the evening.

With a gracious gesture, I pull out the chair for Olivia, my eyes briefly drawn to the back of her gown once more. Subtle lace embroidery adorns the dress, tracing intricate patterns along the neckline, waist, and hem, adding a touch of romantic charm to the overall design. The back of the gown reveals a daring yet tasteful low-cut V framed by a delicate row of covered buttons.

As my fingertips graze the exposed skin on her back, I can't help but revel in how she shudders and how goosebumps rise at my touch.

God, she's so incredibly responsive.

"What can I get you, please?" the waiter asks.

"I will have the chicken soup and steak with a glass of wine," I reply, not bothering to check the menu. I know the menu by heart, having frequented this place for a while now. "What about you, ma'am?" She turns her attention to Olivia, who is currently scanning the menu, obviously perplexed about her choice.

Leaning closer across the table, I ask, "Would you like me to order for you?"

Her shoulders visibly relax with relief. "Yes, please." Glancing up at the waiter, I instruct, "She'll have the same as me but with no tomatoes in the soup."

"Okay. It'll be ready in a few moments," the waiter responds before gracefully departing.

A couple of minutes later, the waiter gracefully places two steaming plates of chicken soup and steak before us. I had requested my steak to be cooked medium, and watching Olivia eagerly cut it into bite-sized pieces and savor it, it seemed like I made the right choice. Her delighted moan sends a shiver down my spine as I sip the chicken soup.

Shifting slightly in my chair, I can't help but ask, "Is it that good?" "Absolutely! This is the best chicken soup and steak I've ever had. How is it so good?" She closes her eyes, humming once more as she savors another bite of the steak.

I smile, my chest swelling with happiness at her enjoyment. "I'm glad you're enjoying it. They have a Michelin star, so I don't expect anything less. It's one of my favorite places to come to when I'm in New York. I'm taking you to my second favorite place after this," I add, my gaze fixed on her.

"Okay," she whispers.

"This is your second favorite place?" Olivia's voice rings with astonishment.

"Yes," I confirm, a hint of a smile on my lips. "Although, technically, it's the first, while the restaurant is the second," I add.

"I never would have pegged you for someone who would like something like this," she remarks, her gaze fixed on the vast fish gracefully swimming in the large glass box within the aquarium.

I can't help but snort. "You thought I was just a boring old man who spent hours in the office and stuck to his job alone?"

"Actually, yes. That's exactly what I thought," she admits with a playful giggle, glancing at me sideways.

"Well, I'm hurt," I say, feigning offense and placing my hand over my chest. "But, sorry to disappoint you. No, I don't spend most of my life stuck behind a desk," I clarify, noticing her raised eyebrow.

"What? I know I've been swamped these days. But I try to make time. When I can." I mumble.

"Sure," she mutters, walking to the right, down to the farthest corner, and gazing at the goldfish in their container.

"Ever since I was young, I've had this weird fascination with sea animals, anything related to the ocean. It always gave me a sense of calm. And I've always wanted to have access to it whenever I wanted, though my job hasn't given me enough time. It's much more convenient than chartering a boat and taking a dunk in the ocean," I explain.

"Wait," she says, straightening her back and craning her neck to look up at me. "Don't tell me you own this aquarium."

I press my tongue against my cheek, taking it lightly and rocking my feet.

"Oh my God," she gasps, her eyes widening. "Is that why this place is empty?" She quickly scans the surroundings.

"Yes." I had ordered the aquarium to be utterly empty tonight. I didn't want it crowded with people; I just wanted a quiet evening with the two of us.

"Wait," she says, straightening her back and craning her neck to look up at me. Her eyes widen with a mix of disbelief and curiosity.

"You own this aquarium."

"Well, come on. There's still a lot I want to show you," I say, reaching out and taking her hand, paying no mind to her shell-shocked expression.

"Wow. I had a great night. Thank you," Olivia breathes out, her face tinged with the flush of the cool night breeze.

"My pleasure," I reply.

However, she hesitates, her lips bitten shyly, eyes cast downward beneath her fluttering lashes. She shuffles her feet upon the floor, leaning lightly against her hotel room door.

"Can I ask you a question?" she says tentatively.

"Of course. What is it?"

"This dinner... Was it truly only to commemorate the finalized deal? Your lawyer should have been in our company. Or was there another motive?" Her question lingers, laden with uncertainty.

Exhaling deeply, I plunge my hands into my pockets. I had foreseen this question, and despite my contemplations, I failed to conjure a credible explanation for the dinner being solely a celebration. Though I acknowledge how selfish it is, I am content to perceive it as a shared date.

"It was indeed a dinner to commemorate the deal. Daniel, regrettably, could not attend," I affirm, my countenance resolute.

"Oh, very well then. Goodnight," she murmurs, turning to leave.

"Olivia," I call out as I take a step closer to her. Her doe-like eyes lift to meet mine.

I'm uncertain of my actions, but the sight of her tongue darting over her crimson-coated lips seals my resolve. I do the one thing I've been yearning to do since I saw her in that captivating dress.

I took a quick step closer, leaning forward; I took her hand and gently pulled her towards me. I bowed my head towards hers, and my lips quickly found hers. A gasp escapes her. I seize the moment to deepen the kiss, thrusting my tongue into her mouth to savor the remnants of the red wine we shared at the aquarium.

I raise one of her legs, wrapping it around my hips, while my hands venture to her soft, ample thighs, gripping them lavishly.

"Wait, wait," she gasps, pulling my lips away and pushing me back.

Breathing heavily and sporting a vast bulge straining through my pants, I wipe my mouth, now tinged with her saliva, and remove the smudge of her red lipstick from my lips.

"What does this mean for us?" she asks, her green eyes piercing mine so intensely that I avert my gaze.

Swallowing hard, I stammer, "I'm sorry. It was a mistake, Olivia. I shouldn't have done that."

A fleeting look of hurt flickers across her face and vanishes so swiftly it could be missed.

"A mistake. Really?" she retorts.

Straightening my shoulders, I utter, "Yes, a mistake," the words grating like gravel in my mouth.

No sooner had I said the words than, sure enough, I felt it. What an ass, and as if telepathic or perhaps by reading my foolish expression, she quickly concurred.

"Of course. What did I expect, anyway? Goodnight, sir," she says before slamming the door in my face.

Damn it!

Chapter 21

Olivia

My brother told me always to date a man who loved me more. He insisted that the depth of my affection was inconsequential compared to his unwavering devotion that being treated like royalty should be the ultimate aim—his words, not mine.

Yet, those words didn't sit comfortably with me.

I yearned for a profound love that could be felt coursing through my veins, a love that would surge through my heart, engulfing my soul and spirit.

I craved it with an intensity that defied reason, a love that would leave me breathless and unshackled.

I craved love– reckless and unbridled.

It might have sounded like something from a fairytale, but I was determined to seek it out.

That's why I steered clear of shallow relationships in Brazil. Crushes may have fluttered through my heart, but none ignited the fire of desire strong enough to lead to a relationship. Observing them from a distance sufficed, and I found contentment in that.

Only two relationships had ever held significance in my life. The first ended because he yearned for physical intimacy, a step I wasn't prepared to take. The second went under when I had to leave for Chicago.

My life resembled a flourishing spring, a meadow teeming with blossoms. Despite our problems, I retained control over certain aspects, particularly heart matters. I could choose whom to like, whom to love, whom to date, and whom to keep at arm's length. It all seemed so straightforward.

That was until I reentered Alexander's life, and he single-handedly dismantled that certainty.

It was infuriating. I crumbled effortlessly at the mere sound of his voice or the simplest gesture. If he were to ask me to fly, I wouldn't question him; I'd only ask, "How high?" It frightened me how much sway he held over my heart.

I was well aware of his sentiments for me, as plain as day. Despite his feigned obliviousness, his feelings were etched clearly in his actions.

And after last night's kiss...

I'd tasted heaven, and despite the numerous glasses of wine I'd indulged in at the aquarium, my head felt lighter.

The kiss in his office had been passionate but impulsive. This, however, was something else entirely. It was intense, primal, and utterly addictive.

Despite my reservations about meaningless relationships, I'd kissed my fair share of men. Yet, none had ever kissed me like that.

It was as though they were conquerors determined to breach my defenses, as if they were lost souls in a desert, and I was their last hope of salvation.

But he had tarnished it all, dismissing it as a mistake. A mistake? Really? Even when I couldn't help but notice the undeniable evidence in his pants?

Enough is enough. I will not allow him to use me, casting me aside at his whim as if I were only good for an occasional kiss and nothing more.

"Oh, what a splendid day to be outside!" I inhale the crisp, clean air of the park, gazing up at the sun-drenched sky as clouds gather overhead.

My decision to leave my hotel room had been last-minute, but not without a careful scan for any signs of Alexander in the hallway. Staying on the same floor, I was determined not to run into him. Not at all.

I feared a single touch from him, and my anger and logic would dissolve like mist in the morning sun.

So, I chose to explore New York alone, even though Alex had offered to show me around. It was his idea to extend our stay in the city by a week, but I relished my independence right now.

Let him do whatever he pleased; I couldn't care less. I'm sure his ego was overcompensating for something else anyway.

Amidst the bustling crowd on the sidewalk, I go to the mall with a specific goal—lingerie shopping.

It was a peculiar fetish of mine, buying and wearing alluring lingerie beneath my everyday attire. It made me feel sexy, like harboring a sultry secret beneath my professional exterior—a secret only I knew.

With two pieces of lingerie, I decided to call it a day and return to the hotel. That's when a familiar voice halts me in my tracks. It was a voice I recognized instantly, sending a shiver down my spine.

"Olivia? I knew it was you!" Gabriel's Hispanic accent greets me, his bright blue eyes sparkling and a wide grin lighting up his face.

"Gabriel? What are you doing here?" I ask, discreetly hiding the Victoria's Secret bag behind my back.

"Wow. After five years, that's the first thing you say to me?" he chuckles, his grin revealing charming dimples.

"It's not like that. I'm just surprised to see you. Last I heard, you were still in Brazil," I explain, my voice softening.

Gabriel was the second man I'd been in a severe relationship with—the one I had to break up with due to the distance, leaving Brazil for Chicago.

I still vividly remember his tearful face during that video call when I explained that a long-distance relationship wasn't fair to him and that he deserved better. It was one of the most complex decisions I'd ever made.

Sliding his hands into his cashmere pants, he says, "There's a lot I want to talk to you about. Would you mind joining me for coffee?"

"Of course," I nod, offering a smile.

Chapter 22

Alexander

"You're going to stare a hole into your phone," Daniel's exasperated voice chides me from across the table.

"Sorry," I mutter, quickly shifting my gaze away from the phone resting on the table.

Daniel sighs audibly, his frustration evident, but he refrains from further comment. "Now, as I said earlier," he resumes, "the Arab prince has stated..."

His words blur into the background.

My eyes involuntarily drift back to my phone, squinting at it slightly, and my restless hands itch to pick it up and make a call.

I promised Olivia I would show her around New York today. I extended our stay by a week just for that purpose.

Yet, I haven't seen her all day.

When I knocked on her hotel room door earlier, it was empty. According to one of the hotel cleaners, she left in the morning. The thought makes my jaw clench with irritation.

Where could she have gone? She knew we had plans today and just left without a word. This childish avoidance infuriates me.

I know she doesn't want to spend time with me, but at least she could have confronted me face-to-face instead of dodging me like a child.

"...And that's the situation. What do you think?" Daniel's voice abruptly pulls me back to the present.

I clear my throat, struggling to refocus. "Yeah, whatever," I reply dismissively.

Daniel straightens up in his chair, staring at me intently. "You weren't listening, were you?"

"No," I admit bluntly.

He sighs deeply. "What's bothering you this time?"

"Nothing in particular. Zoning out has become a part of me. I don't know if it happens to other businessmen, too." I add a chuckle to make light of the situation.

"True, so many thoughts are clogging in."

Daniel's brief laughter ends my quick moment of pretending not to think about Olivia and her whereabouts.

"So, back to business." I sigh, convincing myself that the entire focus of our discussion is mine.

Visible lines of frustration and fatigue freely stretch on Daniel's face as he states all he had said earlier.

"The benefits from the deal were mutual. Although, your company had a fortune from the deal with the Arab prince. The process and outcome are lengthy, but I ensured they provided all hard and soft documents."

"That's great. In conclusion, what's my estimate from the deal?" I ask, hoping we are at the end of the discussion, hoping against all reality for Olivia to walk straight into my arms.

"More than a billion. Almost two," His wry lips parted slowly like the words were as heavy as the money.

A part of my heart feels like it sucked in ecstasy. Business is doing very well; the only sour side is Olivia not showing up, and it is heart-wrenching for a man as old as me to sulk over her.

"It is something." I click my tongue.

"Of course. I will send the papers as soon as I confirm their originality. Have a nice day." He bows slightly.

"We will talk later on, Daniel. Thank you." I wave him goodbye and watch his steady gait as his figure moves away slowly.

I turn to the left, my hands on the railings. The view is quite alluring. Suddenly, I wish it was Olivia and I staring at the clear blue sky and wooly clouds, hand in hand.

A tap on my shoulder jolts me from my wild imagination.

"Oh! Daniel, did you forget something? I did not hear you walking towards me," I turned to see his brown collar shirt.

"Yes, it is an important information I forgot to give." He clears his throat, dropping his suitcase on the table.

"Okay?" I flicker my eyelashes in anticipation. "Why didn't you tell me earlier on?"

"It escaped my mind. And it is something that would be better talked about in person."

"Okay. So, hit me."

"It is about the most..."

My gaze moved toward the laughter that suddenly cut through our conversation. Its familiar tone spells out the name in my head. Olivia.

Then, there is another man, her arms in his—walking side by side, their footsteps exuding harmony. I am likely being overly deep about the courtesy; maybe they are just old friends. She looks too delighted and inarguably beautiful.

The sight of her gives my heart a leap, but at this moment, the presence of her arms tangled with another man's gives me a hot feeling in my ears, like the aftermath of eating raw chili pepper at a Chinese restaurant.

Daniel's gaze followed mine as another outburst of laughter almost echoed in the air. I swallow hard. With her arms in mine, I should be the one who spurs her laughter.

We should be out together looking at the Statue of Liberty, eating cotton candy on the streets, picking wear at the Gucci store. But, here she comes, not alone but with a man.

The urge to make Daniel fade away while I glue my eyes too keenly to see every step she takes, every smile that stretches through her face, and every kiss she would probably steal with that fine young man.

Daniel forced a cough through his throat, purposely returning to our discussion.

"So..." He continues.

"Hmm..." I nod at every word, sharing my consciousness between listening to Daniel and giving a calm look, hoping my forehead isn't lined with any emotion as I watch her.

Chapter 23

Olivia

My eyes widen in surprise as I glimpse Alexander in the lobby. I need the help of no one to tell me his eyes are darting straight at me. He looks like he does not care about who I am with. At the same time, I imagine beads of sweat encroaching on his body, his shirt growing so hot with tiny coals of jealousy.

My grip tightens on Gabriel's arm as we approach Alexander and his lawyer, Daniel. I must have interrupted their meeting with my awkward laughter, and I am not feeling sorry for it.

Last night was a total mess, a dent on me.

Calling the kiss we shared a mistake was unforgivable. I am not a thing to be used and discarded. I am more than an object for gratification.

Words of affirmation fill my head as I hold onto Gabriel a little softer.

"So, it's good to see you again."

"Yeah," I nod, "After a long while."

"You know, I would love for us to start something new. I do not mind starting all over, Liv."

Chuckles of impossibility flew softly out of my closed lips.

He stared at me with pleading eyes, "It can be possible. I do not want to force things. I'll go with whatever you choose for us."

"Oh, well. I understand our past and all that has happened, but we should be friends. I do not hate you. I don't think I like you so much to have you back." I hold his palm, staring into the lines on it like a fortune teller.

Daniel walks past us with unspoken greetings, which we respond to the same way, smiling and nodding briefly.

"I hope the calls will go." It sounds more like a question than a statement.

I nod, "Sure. Certainly." I did not want him to feel thrown out.

"We could still..."

Still in our conversation, a firm hand abruptly drags me.

His grip on my arm makes me feel like a child being pulled away from danger.

Gabriel seemed farther and farther as Alexander yanked me to a corner.

"Just go." My voice squeezed into a whisper.

Gabriel stretches to help, but Alexander's fiery eyes make him withdraw instantly.

"As she said, you can take your leave."

I watch Gabriel's cashmere pants wiggle with his gait. He must feel wrong about Alexander's intrusion—maybe mistaking him for my boyfriend or lover.

My back is pressed against the white wall, and his tall, broad figure stands over me. I prefer this moment with a long, passionate kiss; nevertheless, I do not want emotions to be called mistakes again.

I balance my hurting ankle, pressing my bag in front of me.

"Why did you do that?" I ask,

"Who is that supposed to be?" He pauses,

"First, where did you go? We ought to see around New York—you and I. And suddenly, you disappeared like a ghost. Who does that? Time is precious, Olivia. You should know. A whole week for us to spend good time, away from the pressure and work, and this is how you want to get it started?" He asks, his eyes conveying sadness and a nger.

I stare into his eyes, taking my time to process the replies. I want to be rash, and I also want to be calm—I want to ask if he had forgotten last night. Suppose he sees me as trash if we should act like we are cool after calling a show of love some mistake—so torn between two choices that I just let my mouth choose.

"Do you love me or not? Make it clear that whatever we do is not a mistake. You either accept your feelings for me, or you let me go. The choice is yours, Mr. McQueen." I blurt out.

I did not plan to ask the love question. I needed the truth. Nothing but the truth. I want to be sure that we are on the same page.

I watch as he places his fist on the wall over my head. His mouth moves inaudibly. He knows his feelings but does not want to feel like a simple person.

My gaze follows every movement of his head, searching for answers in his eyes, waiting for a reply.

After what seems like forever, he clears his throat.

"Your elder brother and I have been friends, closer than brothers. You are Camila's best friend. We are more like a family."

"But we are not blood." I cut in.

"I know."

"And then?" I raise my voice to emphasize the question mark behind it. I need a reply more than the friendship ties we have.

"It feels wrong. It just feels wrong. Don't you see what I see?" He asks, holding my hand in his.

"See what you see?" I ask, scoffing. "I see love. Nothing else."

"I'm about twice your age," He widens his eyes.

"Does it matter?"

"It doesn't matter, but it feels like falling in love with a daughter; it is unthinkable, Olivia." He hits his fist a little bit, taking steps away from me.

"Is that all?"

"That is not all. I do not want to make unwise decisions because of emotions. Wrecking friendships will be a huge problem if I say I love you." He drops my hand gently to my sides.

I dig my fingers into my hair. Should the world define what love looks like in situations? I wonder.

Chapter 24

Alexander

Pacing up and down the room for a while is now inevitable as thoughts of Olivia and the growing love for her occupy my mind. Being authentic with oneself is the key to solving a problem.

"Sincerely, I love Olivia. I hate to admit it, but it remains the truth," I mutter, reaching for a glass of water on the bedside table.

I have never thought about a relationship after the terrible incident. A fresh wave of guilt engulfed me on the spot. What is love without loyalty and commitment?

I ease myself into the soft, bouncy, king-sized bed. The gray sheets crumple into sharp lines. For a moment, I feel like pouring all my guilt into the sheets, letting it collapse into strong lines until they disappear.

The constant buzzing of my phone brings my thoughts to a pause. I grab my towel from the wardrobe and enter the scented bathroom.

Every drop of water from the shower convinces me that I love Olivia. The cascading torrent from the shower head transposes images of her cascading waterfall of red hair flowing in the breeze, waving her beautiful vanilla-scented flag across my face, smothering me willingly in its sweet bouquet.

The pearly beads of water coalescing and burrowing a path down my shoulders and across my chest remind me of her bare skin in the sundress and how much I wanted to trace a route between those mountains and valley of soft, supple olive skin, down to the waiting forest below, the mouth of the river of no return, beckoning, yet threatening to swallow me whole.

The bubbles and foam on the water sail helplessly down the drain, leaving the hanging fragrance of a fresh bath and a powerful but helpless man in the grip of something more significant than the sum of its parts. I am a man in love, caught in a snare threatening to end my world. Though I wonder, what would it be without her in it?

I leave the bathroom, wiping my wet feet on the doormat. I imagine myself going to her room to tell her how I feel, though I must explain why I have avoided intimate entanglements and all that comes with it—a secret held for years.

I should see Olivia in a few minutes. I quickly tear a fresh pack of white briefs and throw one on while glancing through my shirts.

I opt for black shorts and a blue T-shirt, misting the air in a sweet cologne that I quickly step through, snaring a little of the vapor to my body so as not to be overpowering. Less is more for an alluring effect rather than hammering her olfactory senses with an onslaught of chemicals that was more typical of young male novices in the arena of intimacy, desperate to conquer their prey. I slide my feet into easy wear, shutting the door after me.

Anxious yet hopeful that everything would go well this time, I knocked on the door to her room after some minutes of hesitation. My heart somersaults as the door opens.

"Hello." She seems to be taken aback.

"Good day, Olivia. Did I disrupt your sleep?"

I cannot help but admire her loosely packed hair and her body in a short, flowery dress. My shower fantasy returns for a few microseconds. My pulse quickens, and that helpless feeling looms on the distant horizon, threatening to pounce.

"Not at all. I wasn't sleeping."

She brushes her hair backward, and my eyes follow the gliding path of her fingers through the strands. Everything drops into slow motion, and a seeming eternity passes in seconds.

"Okay. Do you mind if I come in?"

"No problem. You look cool."

"Thank you."

I grin at the compliment, feeling a modicum of relief and a little more hopeful. I press on. I look younger than my age, so it is a pretty regular thing, but praise from Olivia is a gift of gold to me in this moment of uncertainty.

"I almost assumed you were going somewhere." She sinks into the edge of her bed.

"Right. And I'm here." I reply, wanting to ease the atmosphere.

"You can sit." I breathe in the rosy and sugary scent coming from her as I stand two steps away, ignoring her offer. I don't mind standing closer; I do not want to give mixed signals.

"Err... I'm here to talk about what happened yesterday. I thought about it repeatedly and have decided not to hide my feelings for you.

I love you, Olivia. I do." I admit it.

She stands up from the edge of the bed, eyes wide open, and turns towards me.

I continue..."I also want to say a lot. A lot about me being unable to be in a relationship with anyone."

"But you said you loved me a few seconds ago." She stared boldly right into my eyes.

"Of course I do." I blink, wondering what her point is.

"Then, that will do." She pauses, "I love you too, Alex."

She spreads her arms around me, her tiny fingers locking together as she embraces me. I am also unsure what to do as I wrap my arms around her.

I love her, but she isn't receiving me correctly. There is a lot to this, more to uncover underneath this love.

Her hands slide up my shoulders; she eases onto the tip of her toe. My hands wander down to her waist, holding her so she would not waver. Her chin outstretched, our mouths finding each other. Her supple lips are soft, inviting, and irresistible.

"I want to tell you something..." My words end in her mouth as she slowly kisses me, and I fall further under her spell.

I try to tell her why I am here, but overwhelming emotions envelop her, and her energetic and amorous response pulls me in, but my words can wait.

Like an influence, I find myself taking the lead, kissing her so profoundly as if my life depended on it, and in that very moment, I felt a dam inside give way, then break. The realization slowly dawned on me that this had been building up inside me for a long time. I felt a cascading shower of goosebumps as I reached for her, and our arms touched. Crossing the Rubicon now, there's no turning back for us...

My fingers work their way into her dress, similarly raising hairs on her delicate skin as I attempt to steer her back into the bed. Her breasts open a landscape of possibility as we let ourselves fall into the bed. My mouth grazed her nipples through the flowery fabric en route to Nirvana in our descent, sparking a hidden current of electricity between us. I had longed for this and did not realize how much until now.

I wet her body with kisses; her gasps and subtle moans beckoned me onward, making me crave her more. I am like a hungry man; she is my only source of salvation. After a heated moment, she tore off my shirt, her eyes glowing like a sorceress pulling on me, calling me to her kingdom seductively as she unbuttoned my shirt. I raised my arms in surrender, allowing the removal of my shirt, submitting my all to her will, and followed obediently.

Her fingers trail lines in my back, tickling here and there like keys on a piano, pulling and coaxing me deeper and deeper into her lair. I enter her magical domain and climb higher and higher, through the walls of ecstasy and passion, and she turns over, moving in rhythm with me as she rides me slowly and thoroughly and sets the pace of this enchantment.

Guttural moans escape my throat as sanity rushes from my head, and I climax. She turns to look back at me, the frenzy in her eyes and countenance begging me to thrust in harder and faster. Her soft butt cheeks slap my lap, serving me with continuous growing waves of rhythmic pleasure that send me over the edge.

"Argh..." I moan as the hot liquid fire erupts inside and out of me, seemingly taking all my energy, resolve, and life force.

Half turned, she sits on me and watches me till the very end, eyes wide and hypnotic, dialed in and taking in every second of my euphoria, her hands caressing my thigh, keeping me bound to her, claiming me. Without a doubt, I am hers, entirely undone and under her spell.

I have no idea how many hours we slept, but I blink into reality, seeing us underneath the duvet. Olivia slowly gets out of bed, stretching her limbs, her naked body very visible as my eyes open. Her sexy form hungrily lures me out of bed to follow.

"You are awake." She says, as I wrap my arms around her, my thighs tightened and my morning wood almost touching her lap.

She bends to pick her earrings up from the floor. The side of her butt cheek grazed my flag pole, which is now very awake and at full mast. I sit at the edge of the bed, pulling her over to sit on me.

"You're sweeter than I ever imagined, Liv."

She giggles as I slap her butt playfully. All remembrance of what I had come to tell her the night before had gone from my thoughts. What an excellent way to welcome a new day.

Chapter 25

O*livia*

It is not so bright today, but Alexander and I, on the streets of New York, are enough to brighten up a lifetime with beautiful memories. We walk past artwork of various elements and distinct beauty, artists beckoning us to look at masterpieces that no one has.

The sun seeps out of the clouds at intervals, giving me reasons to see how beautiful New York can be. I admire the crab trailing towards a trash can on the other side of the road until its body shatters into pieces by a red Benz.

"Ouch." I gasp unconsciously.

"Problem?" Alexander asks, holding my hand.

"None. Just a poor crab's demise."
"Okay. And yeah, about crabs. Do you like one?"

"To own?" I lift my left eyebrow.

He brushes a speckle off his shirt, "To eat, young lady."

From my observation, a crab meal is wrong, and puking in a restaurant is missing from my bucket list.

"No, thanks." I smile wryly.

"Do you want to have a taste of the yummiest and cheesiest pizza ever?" He asks cheerfully.

"Of course." I nod in excitement as we walk into a pizza shop.

The aesthetics are excellent. The chairs and tables were beautifully wood-carved with little paintings of cheesy pizza.

"I guess you are in awe of this place," Alexander asks between mouthfuls.

"Of course."

We took a long romantic walk along the East River, then later another lengthy walk towards Central Park, admiring the greenery and trees and the lovely meandering paths taking lovers and families bustling from here to there. The sound of laughter as families come together to picnic and spend quality time outdoors, the joggers and cyclists coming and going.

Alex led us down a hidden path called the "North Woods Trail" on the upper west side. It led to a beautiful secret waterfall, which was secluded and rustic. The absolute highlight of our romantic park meanderings. Right there in the middle of a bustling city. New York had hidden treasures if you had the correct passport. My passport was Alex, and I felt both lucky and blessed.

In our wanderings, we uncovered several other areas, strolling down a main drag called Vanderbilt Avenue in Prospect Heights, a strip of Brooklyn lined with quaint shops, and Prospect Park. We paused briefly at "The Little Cupcake Shop" to sample dessert and visited other neighborhoods and sights, including the Brooklyn Bridge, Queens, and University Place in Manhattan.

Our day winds down as we spend almost two hours at the Gucci shop. We try various designs of hats, sizing boots, and shoes.

"I think this leather jacket suits you. Plus, it's black. Can go with anything." He places a jacket over my shoulders, ushering me towards the mirror.

I cannot help but gasp in approval. "It does suit me. I love it."

"It's yours then." He smiles, hitting me with a loving gaze.

"Thank you." I put my lipstick on.

Every day of the week brings new adventures and new feelings. Being with Alexander forever would be a good idea. Knowing him aside from work, I am surprised at how lovely and loving he is.

****

As I settle into my seat on the flight back to Chicago, I can't help but recall how rough the week started and how smoothly it ended. Accompanying him to New York was a fantastic choice. With the love shared, the city's romance, its beautiful parks and skylines, and his doting presence brought peace and comfort.

Newspapers and magazines clasped in our hands; we are engrossed in the world's stories—a way of staying connected to the pulse of current events, even at 30,000 feet above the ground.

I lower the window shades to gaze out at the fluffy white clouds. The sun behind them almost makes me feel there is a silver lining. I could touch the sky, reach out to God, and grasp his robes.

"It's a heart." I smile inwardly as the clouds move to form irregular shapes.

"I can't see it. I see cotton candy. Like the one we ate at the park." He chuckles, reaching for my hand.

"It was soggy at the end for some unknown reasons." I join in the laugh.

We have been seated for over two hours, and I feel glued to the seat.

"We'll head to the office as soon as we arrive at the airport. It's still early," Alexander whispers into my ears a short while after the announcement of our arrival at the airport.

We roll our suitcase behind us as we approach a black SUV.

"Welcome, sir. How was your trip?" Alexander's driver takes our bags, placing them in the booth.

"Fine, thank you." He replies curtly.

In a few minutes, we arrive at the office. The air smells of coffee, cubicles, papers, and professionalism. I could no longer smell New York, just a slight wafting of Alexander's cologne, brewing coffee, and the iron metallic scent of the word 'work.'

I walk behind Alexander as he waves his hands to the workers whose mouths spew a barrage of morning greetings.

I shut the door behind me, placing some files on his desk. It was pretty dark; the windows were closed, and the curtains were drawn over them. I open one, and a ray of bright light traces a diagonal pattern across the floor and part of the office.

Alexander walks towards me, opening his arms for a warm embrace. I hurry into his arms like a child, swallowing his scent, filling my head, and mapping itself into my memory.

His hand brushes my hair gently. I raise my head to feast my eyes on his handsome, chiseled face.

Our eyes lock momentarily, communicating volumes of unspoken emotions only we understand. He pushed my chin towards him and envelope my mouth with his lips, taking each lip softly, biting it teasingly, pleasurably.

I take a step backward for a second to regain my balance.

"I was wondering if it would end in New York." I suck in my lower lip, still tasting his kiss.

"I don't know either. Maybe Chicago wants some of our love, too." He pulls me closer, locking his lips with mine in a gentle kiss. Coming out of his embrace,

I turned to see a figure seated just a few steps away. I tap Alexander to alert him of my discovery. It isn't Daniel. I do not know what to make from this, but I know this spells trouble.

He stops and turns to where my gaze rests. "Abel!" He mutters under his breath. My head throbs for a split second. I can feel my heart rolling into my throat.

My elder brother Abel is here. This could be better. I can already sense how bad this is going to be. My feet feel stuck and sunken into the marble floor underneath me.

"He didn't see us," I whisper wistfully, trying to convince myself of a new reality where he had not seen our loving kiss and embrace.

Chapter 26

Alexander

My hands feel stiff on her waist. The sweet feeling in my chest slowly turns sour as Abel's gaze tears through me. Shame and guilt soak my insides.

I would welcome being swallowed up by the hungry mouth of the earth than being a victim of Abel's deadly stare. I never knew he would be here. He never called or sent a text message.

My hands feel stiff on her waist. The sweet feeling in my chest slowly turns sour as Abel's gaze tears through me. Shame and guilt soak my insides.

I would welcome being swallowed up by the hungry mouth of the earth than being a victim of Abel's deadly stare. I never knew he would be here. He never called or sent a text message.

His presence makes me feel elated, but today, I feel like a prey watching the predator baring its teeth at me.

I don't know what to say to him. Silence thickens in the air for a long moment, making me uneasy. Abel's stares are like daggers, poisoned daggers. I can feel the intensity of his glare on me. He would plunge them through my heart if he had the chance.

I failed him. I feel disappointed in myself for accepting my feelings for Olivia, his younger sister, after his entrusting me with her, trusting me not to cross boundaries we both knew.

"Are you done?" Abel's husky voice breaks into the silence.

Still in shock, I stutter; no word seems to flow out of my mouth.

"Olivia!" He stands to his feet, strolling towards us.

Maybe my ears played some game with me, but I heard the swallowing of thick saliva down her throat. She must be as devastated as I am, and I blame myself for this.

"I gave warning signs, didn't I, Cara Mia?" His voice softens.

The corner of my eyes reveals Olivia's head nodding in the affirmative.

"And you chose to do the unimaginable?" The edge of his mouth curls, adding a dangerous touch to his soft voice.

"I can talk about it. We can. The three of us." She breathes heavily, breaking away. Her hands hang in the air as she tries to convince him.

I adjust my shirt collar, "Olivia, I want you to leave us." I exhale, wanting to feel calm.

"No," She turns to Abel, "Please, it is not deep. I promise."

"You do not lie to your eyes, or do you?" His face still wears the endless frown, and I cannot tell the degree of his fury.

She holds onto the desk, "No, but we can discuss this without causing a scene. I'm sure it will be a peaceful conversation, and we will reach an agreement."

"Liv, this is not one of your business deals. It is your life. Our life!" He pounds his thigh.

"Abel, please." Her watery eyes will not change a thing between Abel and me.

Tired of watching the two siblings, I tap her back, "Olivia, I would like to have a moment with your brother. Please, excuse us."

Her feet barely move an inch when I bark,

"I said, leave! At this moment." I can no longer control how bad I feel.

I watch Olivia hurry out of our presence, slamming the door after her.

I am standing face to face with my enraged friend whose first sight was beautiful to me yet repulsive to him.

"Abel, you did not tell me you were coming?" I start on a light note, hoping the awkward moment would die in our conversation and the air would be much better to discuss what he had seen.

"How do I have to tell you when you spent your so-called business week with your best friend's sister? With your daughter's best friend?" His fists tighten. His jaw bones clench in fury, and his eyes are sunken and dark.

"Calm down, Abel. I am not taking advantage of her. I would never do that to my best friend's sister. It is a mutual feeling, and I took my time to figure it out. I love Olivia, and she feels the same way." I will explain.

"Really? After all the promises to me? How dare you, Alex?" His voice almost climbs its peak.

"Bro. I need you to chill."

"We made promises, yes or no?"

"We did."

"My sister should never be on your list," He heaves, "Yes or no?"

I keep mute.

"My sister is to be protected by you and not used by you, yes or..."

"I will do no such thing. Use your sister? Man! How do you see me?"

"Do you want us to dig into the past? To see what 'use' is, yeah?"

"Abel, please stop."

"You do things you will regret; why?" He walks away from me, chuckling as he turns an hourglass.

"Abel. I apologize for hurting you, but I genuinely love your sister."

"She is about twice your age, man!" He stomps his left foot.

"Age does not matter." I raise my voice.

"What do you mean?" He hits the desk, rushing towards me with his fist.

My head swirls for a few seconds. I had just received a punch from Abel, his fist so rock hard that blood trickles down my nose.

"Abel. Do not do this!" My rage boils.

"And if I do?" He placed his hands on my arm, launching another punch.

My hand caught his fist mid-air, and I pushed him so hard that he staggered towards the left.

I folded my sleeves, flexing my arms. In a moment when least expected, Abel dashed towards me, throwing me to the ground.

The heat of the scuffle produces numerous beads of sweat. I grunt at each hit, and so does he. Our fists in the air, bruises all over our faces.

Chapter 27

Olivia

Abel's unexpected appearance at the office left me bewildered. The last time we spoke, he had expressed uncertainty about his return to the country, insisting on completing his treatments first. As I glanced at him now, his emotions were a tangled web, no longer as easy to decipher as they were in our youth. His face conveyed shock and a sense of betrayal directed at Alex, who had kissed me in the office.

Alex swiftly dismissed me, his actions betraying an underlying fear, perhaps more significant than his love for me. He ushered me out of the office, attempting to calm Abel. But Abel remained resolute, backing away as Alex approached. He shot Alex an accusing look before letting out his pent-up frustration.

"How could you do this to me?" Abel's voice thundered in the hallway. "I trusted you," he added, his voice quivering with anger and disappointment.

"Abel, please, let's discuss this rationally," Alex implored, desperation creeping into his voice.

"Discuss what? The fact that you're having an affair with my kid's sister? Someone the same age as your daughter?" Abel retorted, his rage intensifying as he knocked a system off his desk, sending it crashing to the floor.

The commotion had drawn the attention of everyone in the hallway. Some stood frozen, while others huddled in small groups, whispering words I couldn't discern. A few remained unfazed by the unfolding drama.

I couldn't bear to face them. It was evident that they had concluded I was the cause of this office turmoil, and I couldn't blame them. I blamed myself for falling so recklessly for Alex.

Abel's voice grew quieter, prompting me to inch closer to the office door, straining to hear through the slight opening in the curtain that covered the glass partition.

Abel stood with arms folded, glaring at Alex. Alex muttered something inaudible to me in an attempt to appease Abel. His voice was barely audible.

"Shut up, you fool!" Abel erupted, his fists clenched, poised for a physical confrontation.

"After all we've been through, our shared experiences as young teens. And you betray me like this. Can you brush it aside, claiming you don't know how it happened?" Alex's voice grew firmer, laced with mounting anger.

I had to intervene before Abel inflicted harm on Alex. The tension was palpable, and Alex, once confident, now exuded fear.

I pounded on the door and shouted, pleading with Abel to calm down. "Please, Abel, don't hurt him. I love him."

"Shut your mouth! You've brought disgrace to our family with what you've done!" Abel shot back, his anger unabated.

"Please..."

"Abel, let's talk...release him," I implored, my voice shaking. I continued to pound and kick the door, but it remained unyielding.

Abel's fist struck Alex's face, causing him to stagger backward. Then, like a torrent, the blows rained down on Alex, from his face to his jaw, eyelids, and abdomen. Alex tried to defend himself, but his efforts were futile. Abel's relentless assault continued until Alex crumpled to the floor, exhausted and battered.

"Let me catch you kissing my sister again!" Abel declared, his tone carrying an air of finality.

Abel finally withdrew, swinging the office door wide open. He forcibly pulled me out of the building and into the car, swearing to deal with me once we got home.

My heart ached for Alex; he didn't deserve this treatment. It was the price of the love that had found us.

Abel's shouts persisted as he drove, but their words faded into a distant blur. Lost in my thoughts, I wondered how Alex would cope with his injuries and what the next few hours or days would be like for us.

Tears streamed down my cheeks as Abel continued to shout and strike the steering wheel like a madman. My whole world had flipped upside down—one minute, a bed of roses; the next, carnage.

Chapter 28

Alexander

I lay on the floor with body aches all over. I hadn't sustained such heavy kicks or blows simultaneously in a very long time. My pleas to Abel had all fallen on deaf ears like water off a duck's back. I had pleaded, but each request came with even heavier blows as I struggled to stand.

Yes, I was in love with the sister I never thought I would ever be ...Seeing the circumstances surrounding our work, falling in love couldn't be avoided. It was just a matter of time.

We had a history; we were already close and emotionally connected because we were almost family. And since we were always working nearby, sometimes late at night. She served the best coffee, made sharp, acute observations, provided genuine feedback and sound advice, and was smart and funny. She was with me on all my business ventures. I couldn't help but fall in love with her. She was intelligent, hardworking, and the perfect assistant I would want to have at work. And what's more, she was a beautiful, selfless soul with intelligence and charm to spa re.

I could hear Abel's car zoom off almost immediately as he left the building. I groaned and rolled in pain as I tried to get up.

My ankles were bruised with his boot imprints. I couldn't move my body the way I would have wanted. I pulled up to my office chair and tried to get a hold of myself as I sat down.

A few hours passed, but mercifully, no one came to check my condition. The door was closed, and the noises of the fight scared everyone off enough for them not to risk my ire by entering unbidden. I was a grown man, the boss. I could take care of myself.

It was already late, and all my workers had gone home for the day. I had to nurse my wounds, which had already become lumps on my face. No, I couldn't go home this way. How do I explain how this happened? My daughter Camilla would quickly know if I were to be lying. She easily reads me like a book these days, no matter how smart I try to play on her.

Two things were certain from tonight's incident: Olivia would get sacked or placed in another department far from me. To avoid a repeat of Abel's untimely visit, not to mention the pain of my disappointing him and, of course, the kicks and blows that followed. This was my resolution, and I was firm on it.

I took some ice cubes from the refrigerator near my office desk. I took turns placing it on my temples, lower and upper jaw, and then my shoulders, where the kicks were felt the most. I was still in the process of doing this when I heard the sound of a door opening.

I panicked and quickly shuffled the ice cubes into the fridge as I made my way to hide. Maybe Abel had finally decided to finish me off so he wouldn't see me as a threat near his sister again. I began to mutter my last words while waiting for Abel to bang through my door and take my head off.

After a while, I heard no sound or anyone coming, so I slowly crept out of my hiding spot.

I went round the office block and found no one. I heaved a sigh of relief, returned to my office, and returned the ice cubes from where I shuffled them. Just as I repeated placing the ice cubes on my affected regions. The office door burst open.

Startled by the sudden movement, I dropped the ice cubes. They fell from my hands and clattered to the floor.

I looked closer, only to see Olivia approaching the office desk.

"What are you doing back here?" I asked with a look of discontentment on my face.

"I came to tend after your wounds," she said with her face all sad and expressionless at the same time.

"Oh, you've come to have me killed, right? No thanks." I shoved her off as she approached closer

"Please let me handle it."

"I'm doing fine with it already. You can leave."

"I don't want to go," she said with her eyes on me

"Olivia, you have to let me go. We can't have this relationship, please. Leave my office now!"

She looked at me, stunned, before once again pleading with me.

"I'm sorry it had to be like this. I had no idea he was in the country."

"It was none of your fault... now please go."

She looked pleadingly at me, then finally took her bag and left.

I watched her from my office window, giving a full view of the city's landscape. She glanced up from below for a moment. After a while, she stopped the next taxi going her way and left my sight.

Chapter 29

Olivia

The following week could have been faster. It began with the rudest shock when I came to work and wasn't allowed entrance into the office building.

"What's the meaning of this?" I shouted at the security man who had always been my friend.

"Please, ma'am, Mr. Alexander instructed me not to allow you into the office premises."

"For how long?"

"I don't know, ma'am. He just instructed me not to let you in," he said and bent his face almost immediately.

"Did he make this decision because of what happened last week? Please tell me the truth," I asked.

"I truly don't know, ma," he answered back

"Then I have to see him for myself."

"I'm sorry, but you can't do that," he said with his face up and giving me a stern look this time.

This was serious, and I might miss work for the whole week.

I went home afterward

Abel was about to make breakfast when I stepped in

"What happened? Why are you home so early?" He asked just before I placed my handbag on the kitchen counter

"You expect he will let me into the office premises after all you did to him?" I returned his question with a bigger one

"Well, I had to do what had to be done."

"Which is?"

"Save you from him."

"I don't need anyone to save me. I have been coping well all these years without you."

He placed the bacon and eggs on the table before undoing his apron.

"Care for some?" He asked before sitting down

"No, thank you. I'm okay." I waved my hand off before getting a soda from the fridge.

"Olivia, you're my kid, sis. And my responsibility as well. So don't get mad when I say that." I need to save you from him." "

"Why do you feel you need to? Because he is old, and I can't be with someone that old?"

"No, not that." he adjusted his eggs before cutting through

"All I'm saying is that. I've known Alex since we were kids, and he isn't the best option for you." he leaned back from his seat and looked at me.

"You're not being honest. You're just trying to fight him off because he is your friend and because everyone thinks it's a forbidden kind of affair."

"Yes, it is forbidden. But I don't have the right to your love preference. You can marry someone twice your age; that's not my business. But not Alex."

"Not Alex? What has he done that has made you detest him so much?"

"I don't detest him, Olivia; we've been friends since childhood."

"I doubt you'll remain friends after putting him in that situation."

"What situation? He is my friend, after all, and he will surely come around," he boasted in his confidence.

"You sound so sure."

"Yes, I am sure." he smiled this time just as he finished his meal.

"Abel, can you tell me exactly? Why don't you want me and Alexander together?"

"He is not the right man for you... there are many guys out there. Alex is just not the one for you".

"That's not concrete enough, and you know it. I need more answers!"

But I have yet to get any. He smiled at me and walked out of the dining room.

I worried about Camila; I hadn't spoken to her all week. What would she do if she knew about my illicit affair with her dad? Someone was bound to tell her the next time she went to the office to see him as she sometimes did to take him for lunch.

Suddenly, we seemed so distant, and I longed to talk to her again. I called her later, but her number wasn't going through. The timing was unsettling. Could this be a coincidence?

Alex had been on my mind ever since I stopped working. I wanted to see how his wounds were now. Despite pushing me out the other day, I still felt drawn to him.

His eyes showed that of a wounded lion when I came to look after his wounds that night. He seemed so withdrawn, like I was about to lynch an attack on him.

I called him, but his words were sharp and straight.

"I don't want you near the office for the whole week," he said over the phone, his voice showing no emotion.

"Is this about what happened last week?" I tried to chip in over the call.

He kept quiet for a moment, as though he was about to break down, and finally said, "No. Just don't come to the office the rest of the week," he said with that same sharp tone.

"We can talk about this," I said, trying to talk him out of his resolution.

"There is nothing to talk about. See you next week!" he said before hanging up.

I stared into the blank space for a while and wondered how it hurt so much to be in love.

Chapter 30

Alexander

Working without Olivia seemed like carrying a big mountain at my back. I had to do double time on each of my appointments.

Even though I got someone to replace Olivia, the lady was slow and sluggish. Her coffee left much to be desired. Either the milk was excessive, or the sugar was insignificant. She was never really able to maintain a consistent dosage of milk and sugar.

I longed now to see Olivia's beautiful face with its youth and glamour, no matter how much I felt drawn to her. I couldn't give in to calling her to come back to work.

I wanted her to stay far away from me, and, at the same time, I tried to keep her close to me. So conflicted was my world. I cannot be with her and cannot live without her: the agony and the ecstasy.

During official meetings or conferences, my mind was usually absent from what was being discussed; some of my friends noticed and asked what was wrong, but I shoved it off and assured them everything was great.

My work lost meaning to me, and I began to spend more time at the bar while my manager and lawyer handled my business affairs.

It was better to get drowned in alcohol than worry over some woman who haunted my waking hours and wouldn't let me have a moment's peace or concentrate at work.

"Why must I be so involved?" I whispered as I gulped the remaining contents of my glass. "Why can't I get her out of my mind?"

"Sir, you've taken much drink today. Don't you think you should pause for a while?" Said the young waitresses whose eyes shone so brightly.

"Will you keep it shut, young girl! ... Don't I pay for the drinks?"

"You do, sir, but you shouldn't get so undone because of love... I overheard your whisper."

"What do you know about love... tell me, young lass, tell me. I want to know. Since you claim to be so smart".

"My apologies, sir. I know nothing about love." The girl quickly bends her head down before leaving.

"Get me more Beer!" I shouted from my seat to the waitress, who was already leaving.

"Yes, sir," she answered.

My phone began to buzz, and behold, it was Camilla who was calling

"Hi, Dad, where are you?" Camilla's voice rang out loudly, making my head spin

"I'm at the bar," I said, trying to gain composure of myself

"Bar? I thought you had some important project going on with Daniel. Besides, it's 1 pm. Lunchtime. How is it you are at the bar so early?"

"I needed to clear my head... my manager and lawyer can handle everything. That's why I am the CEO." I prided myself on my achievement

"Dad, they are competent, but that's not the point. You must look out for our interests; you still can't trust them with everything."

"Oh no, I do. You don't need to worry. What are they going to do? Sell the company?" I boasted again.

"Anyways, what bar are you at? I'm coming to pick you up. I can't have you being drunk in the afternoon; what if someone recognizes you and takes a picture? The newspapers would have a field day."

"I'm not drunk, Camilla. Don't you worry about me; I'll be fine." I tried to defend myself, but she would have none of it.

"Dad, I'm still waiting... What bar are you at?" she persisted with the question.

"Meet me at Swiss bar."

"Okay, Dad... see you in 5," she said before she hung up

Camila walked into the bar exactly 5mins after the call

"Hi, Dad,"

"Hello honey, how are you?" I answered while taking a long shot of whiskey

"Okay... you have to stop now," she said while dragging the bottle of whiskey out of my hand.

"Stop what? This is the only thing that makes any sense to me now," I said while trying to grab the drink away from her, but she had shifted it far from me.

My legs were too weak to stand up and get the bottle back, so I gave up

"What's wrong, Dad? Why are you drowning yourself in whiskey?" she said, trying to get me to talk.

"Camila, you wouldn't understand. This is a matter of the heart," I responded with no enthusiasm.

"You mean love is what has got you like this? Dad, you're in love?" She said with a look of shock and disbelief in her eyes

"Yes, I am. What's so hard to believe?"

"Not like I disbelieve that you're in love, but I'm surprised and shocked that you allowed it to get to you like this."

"What do you mean?" I said

"Dad, all I'm trying to say is that. It's okay to love anyone you wish. Go all in, all out, fully to love them, and show them how much you care, and if it doesn't work out, then know you did your best. No regrets"

"Really?"

"Yes, Dad, I'm in full support of you having a love life and a life and happiness of your own, and please don't allow anyone to get you down this way... you're charming, handsome, and a wonderful father. A CEO to boot, Dad. That doesn't stop you from having a love interest," she said, with her words of wisdom flowing easily.

"Okay, Camila... thank you for this. I needed this"

"You're welcome, dad. You know I've got your six, always. Now come, let's go home; I have made a special delicacy for you," she beamed with a broad smile.

"Of course," I said as I thought about my jacket.... I paid the servers the rest of my bills and went home in the care of my very wise and grown-up daughter.

Chapter 31

Olivia

"I do not want you near my sister if you are going to lie to her," I hear Abel half yell at Alex. They have been at it for about ten minutes, and the night of their scuffling keeps repeating.

"Don't touch her, and let me explain to her."

I would have gone to separate them, but they both got on my nerves.

Why would Alex yell at me like I was a child? Maybe he would not see me as someone mature enough for him, and it hurt. I just wanted him to stop thinking about me like I was a kid. He is already attracted to me, so why the faking?

"I want to tell her the truth." I heard Alex say, and I raised my head to look at them from the window.

"You want to?" My brother's voice was now less rigid and softer. What were they talking about?

"Yes. There is no need to lie or hide. If she wants me, she will take me." Alex said to my brother, who stood there, still shocked.

"And if she eventually wishes to stay, please don't stop her from it. I will not be irresponsible this time. I promise." Alex says with all seriousness and humility.

I have never seen him that serious. And that was when it dawned on me that whatever secret he had could break me. Did he hurt someone or kill someone?

What could make my brother, his best friend, angry with our relationship? Many questions were running through my mind.

Will I be able to look at him the same way, or would I unthinkingly drive past even when the red light is glaring? I had so many questions, and only one man could answer them.

I closed my eyes, took a deep breath, and heard the door open. I opened my eyes and sat up straight, meeting eyes with Alex as he walked in.

I looked towards the door, which was swinging closed, and then saw my brother; I was unsure if he was coming or going before the door swung shut.

"Hey," said Alex, apprehensively as he neared me.

"Hi," I didn't bother acting like I was still upset.

"I am sorry I yelled at you. It was just too much at the moment." He said, and I blinked a nod of understanding.

Even when he was at his meanest, he would not yell without cause, and I appreciated that he always accepted his faults, but this was a very mean thing to do. He went as far as sending me out of the company without even a note of explanation.

"The company?" I asked, and he just looked down at the floor contritely.

"Well, I am sorry about that too. I should have gone about it more maturely. I needed space and wanted to take it without you telling me it was a mistake," he explained, and I just nodded. He already accepted, and that was what mattered.

"So you have something to tell me?" I said, going straight to the point of why he was here.

"Yes, I do," he said nothing else, and I did not, too, for a few minutes. We both were looking into space. I was seated here on the couch in my house, noticing the torn line in it for the first time. Life was something.

"You know you can tell me anything bothering you, right?" He said, and I nodded.

"Yes, I know I can. But what should I be telling you right now? I was not sure if you were the right one for me. That I was already doubting my feelings for you? Or that everything is making me anxious, including how you keep swinging your legs back and forth."

"I...I" gosh!

"Alexander, please just say it, whatever it is, the big secret. All of this is making me extraordinarily anxious."

He nodded and opened his mouth. "I killed someone."

Chapter 32

Alexander

She gasped, putting her hand to her mouth and walking out. Gosh, I did not bother stopping the tears threatening to flow.

I called after her and risked following her when she didn't answer. As I walked in the direction she had gone, I heard her puking her guts out, making me run to her, holding her hair and rubbing her back.

"Please listen to it all before you judge me," I told her. I did not care for anyone judging me and my decisions.

"You killed someone. I don't know," she said as she raised her head from the toilet seat.

I helped her up and held her as she worked to the sink to wash her face.

I stood quietly as she did everything with so much apprehension and nervousness. When she was done, we both moved to the sitting room and back to the couch we had been seated before.

"Tell me everything," she said. I stretched my hands to touch her, and she refused, keeping her hand to herself, so I sat down instead.

"A few years ago, I dated this girl; she was beautiful and younger than I am. I was careless, boastful, and had much pride.

Despite her plea and conviction that it was mine, I got her pregnant and denied the baby. I could not have a child at that time.

One day, I was drinking, and she kept calling, but to this day, I cannot remember what we talked about. The next morning, I heard she died, and I was arrested. Thankfully, I had an alibi and a camera witness.

She had died that night. I was sure I had said something mean, or maybe I told her to kill herself. She died. Because of me."

I eventually finished telling my story, and I could not help the tears that flowed. I had tried to remember a million times, but I never did. And I hoped the day I finally did would not destroy me beyond expectations.

"This is a lot." That was all she said as she looked at me with the same pity everyone did that day.

"I know. I am sorry. Whatever happened between us was not a mistake or some form of redemption, so don't think that." I told her. I didn't want her to think I used her to pay for my sins.

I had stayed without anyone; I was taking care of my daughter. I will hold on to Olivia until she wants me to let go.

"I don't know," that was all she kept repeating for a few minutes. I just nodded.

"I know it's hard to understand. But I hope you will be able to get past it.

Whatever your decision is, I will be here for you, and I will accept it," I said to her and made to stand up, but she held my hand.

I looked into her eyes and noticed it was dropping, so I carried her and headed to her room. After dropping her on her bed, I waited for her to sleep off before covering her properly and walking out.

I was super stressed and anxious.

Just thirty minutes after getting home, I went directly to the fridge for a cold beer when I heard a knock at the door.

I was skeptical about who it was, but as I checked through the camera, I noticed it was Abel. What was he doing here?

I groaned because I was not ready to receive another punch.

"Waassup... man," was the first thing he said as he pulled open the door. I smiled, shaking my hand, but he pulled me in for a hug.

"Can I get a beer?" he said, and I nodded, welcoming him in.

"So what are you doing here?" I asked him. He opened the beer and took a sip, putting it down and seating himself.

"It's about my sister, man."

"I already told her everything, and I do not plan on forcing her to do anything, but if she stays, I will be with her throughout it," I told him before he continued.

"You know how precious she is to me, and I want you to treat her like that. I don't want my sister to create an issue between us. I told her the same thing, man.

Please treat her right." He said. Abel rarely pleaded, and I knew this was hard for him to say, but it was needed.

"Yes, man. I promise," I told him, and he hit my arm lightly.

"The same way you promised to stay away." We laughed over it and continued catching up until he left a few hours later.

Chapter 33

Olivia's

I woke up this morning extraordinarily nauseous and knew there was a problem, so I rushed to the pharmacist to get a test kit for pregnancy. It was highly possible.

As I opened the door to my house, my brother was the first person I met. Fuck!

"Where are you coming from?" He asked me, probably suspecting the way I quickly hid the bag.

"The store," I told him and briskly walked away.

"Wait, Olivia," he said and halted before turning confused and scared he had caught me.

"What?" I asked him, and he turned to me

"I spoke to Alex yesterday. And I realized that I was being selfish.

Indeed, what he did was wrong, but he didn't kill her. His only fault was neglecting her, which was terrible. And he has paid for it severely.

I hope you guys make yourselves happy if you forgive him. But if not," he said and turned back to the TV like he had not just given me the most precious speech of all those he had given me previously.

"Thank you, brother." If it were some other day, I would disturb him, but today I had another mission. I hurried to the toilet, locking the door and double-checking that it was closed.

Finding a cup in the sink, I peed in it and took the test. I waited with apprehension and then screamed in relief as I saw the result. I was pregnant.

"Is everything okay, Oli?" I heard my brother say, and I nodded.

"Yes, I'm fine," I wanted to tell Alex first.

"Ok," he said gruffly, and I heard as his feet shuffled off. I threw away every piece of evidence and took the test strip out of the toilet. I walked to my room to get dressed.

****

"Hey," I greeted Alex as he opened the door. It looked like he had a rough night and was waking up, and I confirmed that when I saw bottles lying around.

"Did you drink all this?" I asked, surprised. He was not much of a drinker; I could confirm that.

"No, your brother came over," and I nodded. Abel was a borderline drunk. Thank goodness he was responsible for it.

"Seems you had fun," I told him as I sat. He sat opposite me on the table and sighed.

"Yes, I did, but I was apprehensive about you."

"Okay. I have thought about what you said yesterday, and Abel also helped me put it into perspective.

You did not kill her; yes, you were irresponsible, but you did not kill her. You should stop blaming yourself, you know?

So I want to let you know that since my brother and your daughter, who has not called me or picked up my calls, are in favor, I am here."

I told him to go straight to the point. Now I know why I felt relieved when I discovered I was pregnant. I truly loved him.

"I love you." I quickly added that before he could say anything. "...and I have something important to tell you."

"Awww.... aw so cute," I heard my best friend say, and I looked up at the source, which quickly turned to a glare.

"Why have you not been picking up my calls?" I asked her.

"I just did not want you making a decision based on my influence." She said, and I understood.

"Okay, since you are still in shock, I might as well go all in. In for a penny, in for a pound. I have news for you both. Since you are both the closest family to me and are the dearest persons in my life, besides Abel, of course. You should know that I am pregnant." I said.

"Gross," my friend cut me off, making me laugh. I pulled out the result and handed it to Alex. He looked at me, frozen to the spot, and then his expression broke into a warm grin, with tears running down his eyes as my friend jumped around everywhere in response to his reaction, squeaking out her expressions of joy.

"I'm going to be a big sister."

He stood up and lifted me off the ground, his eyes shining with love, as he embraced me, and I felt all the words he could not speak. His passion for me poured out of him like a fountain, and I was grateful. Family. These are my loves, and this is my life. I am so blessed.

The End.

If you enjoyed this book

If you enjoyed this book, you will also like my new book

A Billionaire Tryst

By

Neve Star

===

The first rule of the bodyguard business: never screw your client,

especially if she's a walking disaster waiting to happen.

Fresh off a broken heart, I banged this Hollywood siren who'd just dumped her boyfriend.

Even though we nearly broke the bathroom stall back then, now, years later, we meet and

I don't recognize her.

Her life's threatened. She's back and thinks I'm a cold fish.

There's more to me than that, so I'll be professional and keep her safe.

Stuck on an island, I realize she's genuine and smoking hot.

If news of me sleeping with my Ward gets out, the publicity will surely ruin me.

Had I recognized her sooner and not stepped in this GIANT steaming pile of...

I wouldn't risk her life, my business, and my family's reputation.

This secret could free us to fall in love or tear everything apart.

Whatever happens, I'll protect her, even if it costs me everything.

A Billionaire Tryst - Sneek Peek

A Billionaire Tryst

Prologue

Celia

"You know, for a woman who tries to prove to the world that you've got your shit together, you sure ain't fooling me." Justin's levelly baritone voice and deep Southern accent grate against my nerves as he points out one of my many failures as a Hollywood starlet.

"Screw you, Justin! And get the hell out of my apartment!" I snapped at him, resisting the urge to throw him out physically. His tall, imposing figure was one other thing that held me back.

He was at least 6'2, while I, barely 5'2, dwarfed him by a mile. He could flick me off with a finger, and I did not want to test the theory of whether he was one of those guys who could get angry enough to hit a woman.

"Gladly!" He snapped back, raising both hands as if in gratitude to the universe that he was finally free of me, and then the next thing I heard was the loud slam of the door shutting behind his exit.

"Son of a ...!"

I looked around the apartment, which was currently in disarray, and cursed out loud. I hated being on my own, hated being alone in this godforsaken town. Here, being alone felt like a disease, a one-way road into the fiery pits of depression, and if you didn't have anyone you could trust around you, then you had pills, or alcohol, or some fake ass fellowship bullshit that people only go to to make themselves feel better about their horrible lives.

My vice was using people to escape the funk of loneliness. It had been a plague I'd been born with all my life. I was abandoned at a church and grew up in an orphanage with no friends, even though other girls like me had been plenty. For some reason, girls saw me, and the first thing they thought about was competition. I had my looks to blame for it,

I was a fiery redhead with sparkling piercing blue eyes that were big, round, and, like many of my ex-boyfriends would say, Intense. And most of them would say I had the personality to match.

Justin and I had been dating for almost a year, and like most of our fights, I could not even remember the details of what led to this particular fight. All I know is that we looked for reasons to chew each other out, and then we would reconcile in the most explosive ways, screwing around like bunnies and being all lovey-dovey with each other for the next few weeks. And then something else would come up like he could not keep his eyes from wandering and his hands to himself. I think we only stay together for the make-up sex.

I was a jealous lover; I was not one of those Hollywood princesses who could look the other way while their boyfriends did whatever they liked and then smiled in front of the cameras like they were the most loved-up couple. I could not do that; it gave my agent a most painful headache daily, and the poor chap was probably tired of me.

At just twenty-three, I attained a level of success in the industry that even I had never dreamed of. I had run away from my foster home the day after I clocked eighteen, just two weeks after my high school graduation, and made the short trip from a small town in Arizona to Los Angeles. It did not take long for me to land a modeling gig thanks to my young age, good looks, and body.

I had barely worked as a waitress for scarcely a month before I could afford my rent, and I moved out of the communal home I'd been living in. I had started to get minor commercial roles until I was scouted by my now-current agent, Hal Garrison.

He had pulled a few strings that had landed me my first significant role after only three months of taking acting classes. I'd taken to the part like a moth to a flame, and before I knew it, my face was on billboards on Hollywood boulevards, I was stepping out of limos at award shows and being asked whom I was wearing, and my career had kicked off from there.

However, I had a bad habit of dating my co-stars, which made me somewhat controversial in the eyes of the tabloids. Hal always said every kind of publicity, bad or good, was good publicity, but I did not want to be known as sensational; I wanted to be known for my work as an actor, even though most times I found it hard to separate my work feelings from real life feelings.

This brought me back to Justin Skyler, my on-again, off-again boyfriend whom I had met on my new show, 'Enchanted.'

I was a dragon princess trying to master my powers of dragon mind control, while Justin was a co-star and love interest, helping me every step of the way.

We had been barely three weeks into shooting before we started hooking up, and even though we tried to keep it from the producers, someone had leaked it, and then our still-growing relationship had been milked for all it was worth to promote the show.

We had broken up at least three times while filming, but we always came back together, and I knew even now it would not be long before Justin would call, cringing for me to take him back.

Sick and tired of my own company, even though it was barely ten minutes since Justin stormed out of my apartment, I left the building to where my car was parked and sneaked out without alerting my bodyguard.

I was getting tired of the unending cycle and did not know how much more my heart could take being disappointed by Justin before I decided to move on from him. There were very few sincere men in this industry, and it was almost impossible to meet someone who was not an actor, a studio exec, or his son.

I'd tried dating a guy who was not an actor once, about two years ago; he had been a stunt double who also doubled as a busboy at a cafe I liked to frequent. Charming and hot with a beautiful smile that put young Leonardo Di Caprio to shame, I'd fallen so hard and fast I almost lost sight of anything but him.

But like most people, he had only been using me to get ahead, and when I caught him making out with his fellow actress in the car I'd bought for him as a gift, that was the end.

I had my heart broken too many times to count, and I was getting sick and tired of the circle since it did not seem to be ending anytime soon.

Could you stop dating?

A part of my brain whispered to me, but I ignored the advice and drove into the parking lot of what looked like a seedy bar along the road. It was barely late, around nine thirty pm, and I had to be on set the following day, but I could not bear the silence of my apartment and the loud voices in my head of my own company. I needed the distraction.

I fetch a blonde wig from the glove compartment, my usual disguise, whenever I go out alone, and swipe on a wig cap over my red mop of hair, fixing the blonde wig over it. And then fetch my sun shades from my purse and put them over my eyes.

Staring at my reflection in the mirror does very little to cover my identity, but it has to do. I am wearing a short dress with heels that cost more than a few month's rent for some people in that bar, but I have my bodyguard on speed dial if I need him.

Hopefully, it will not come to that.

The bar is a little rowdy when I walk in, and I note there are as many women in it as there are men, which calms me down a little. Keeping my head down, I walk through the multitude of people to the bar. There are two servers behind the counter trying to beat the rush, and being an expert at this, I whistle to catch the hot guy's attention, who gives me a broad smile and immediately serves up my drink, a dry martini.

Holding the tiny stem glass in my hand, I turn around to give the room a slight perusal, but nothing holds my interest for long, so I turn back to my drink and take another sip, emptying the glass in one long swoop and ordering two more.

Feeling heavy eyes on my arms covered in goosebumps, I stare across the bar table and find a pair of intense gray-green eyes staring back at me from thick, beautifully arched lashes. Kind of a modern-day Paul Newman look-a-like if you are familiar with classic Hollywood stars from the earlier times or the Butch Cassidy & Sundance films, except that he has an intriguing-looking tattoo on his arm. Heat flashes through me, white-hot and aggressive, and I am riveted.

The man is as hot as sin with a body build that would make a gym trainer envious, thick dark hair that begged me to run my fingers through and a straight-set jawline that you could probably sharpen a pencil on.

My tongue darts to lick my lower lips as I give him a come-hither smile so he does not fail to take the bait.

My heart starts pounding as I watch him stand to his full height and approach me.

He was tall. A definite 6'2 or more, with broad shoulders and bulging muscles, but not so buff that he looked hooked on steroids. He had a swimmer's build. Muscled but lean, I had to rub my thighs together to ease the pressure that builds between my legs.

"Hello," I speak to him first once he is close enough to hear, and he does not crack a smile; his eyes are red, a little bloodshot, and very intense. I sensed that he was going through something, maybe a loss or a heartbreak, and like me, he was here because he needed a distraction.

I was very good at distractions.

"You look like you could use a friend or maybe a good distraction," I tell him, dropping my voice a few decibels lower than usual into a whisper to bring him closer and reel him in.

It works like magic when I see his eyes darken even more, and he sets his drink glass right next to mine.

"Are you offering?" he asked,

He had a deep voice and a New York accent from the little I could detect. I don't waste time before I smile and nod, and the next thing I know, I am being led by the end toward the bar's backroom.

I have no idea how he has access, and I knew I was probably making a big mistake, but I was too blinded by the rushing chemistry of lust and a broken heart to listen to the voice of reason.

He walks through a darkened hallway into a dimly lit bathroom and slams the door shut behind me, slamming my back against it and crashing his lips down to mine.

He tasted of liquor and all-male, and my hands sifted through his dark hair to grab fistfuls.

"Do you have a condom?" My brain function kicks in long enough for me to ask, and he growls against my mouth, his hands fishing into his back pocket to grab one and show me.

"Good. Now, fuck me."

Get

A Billionaire Tryst

============================

"A Billionaire Trust."

If you enjoyed those books and still can't get enough, you would definitely like my next book...

"A Billionaire Trust."

Ashley Turner runs into Xander Haynes at her friend's wedding. Xander had been friends with her older brother, Jonah, in high school. He moved to New York to study medicine and belonged to a wealthy family. He is a renowned surgeon in New York.

Meanwhile, Ashley is a schoolteacher and works at the local middle school. She is also a genius with children, and has discovered a revolutionary way to save lives in the way she works with them. She has had a major crush on Xander in high school, but he didn't notice her. He barely recognizes her at the wedding since she looks very different.

===

Coming Soon

Free on Amazon Kindle Unlimitedin 2024

==

SIGN UP FOR MY NEWSLETTER

♥

Sign up for my newsletter

By signing up you will be notified of my next release.

And when you sign up, you can download your

FREE COPY

Of my book

"A Billionaire Secret."

Click Here

For Paperback Readers, email a request to join my newsletter at Hello@nevestarromance.com

===

Manufactured by Amazon.ca
Bolton, ON

38080490R00125